TOSSED
into LOVE

Shooting Stars Series

Fighting to Breathe
Wide Open Spaces
One Last Wish (coming soon)

Fluke My Life Series

Running Into Love
Stumbling Into Love
Tossed Into Love
Drawn Into Love (coming soon)

Ruby Falls Series

Falling Fast

Writing as C.A Rose

Alfha Law Series

Justified
Liability
Verdict (coming soon)

Stand-Alone Titles

Finders Keepers

TOSSED
into LOVE

Aurora Rose Reynolds

Montlake
Romance

Published by Montlake Romance, Seattle

www.apub.com

Amazon, the Amazon logo, and Montlake Romance are trademarks of Amazon.com, Inc., or its affiliates.

ISBN-13: 9781503905467
ISBN-10: 1503905462

Cover design by Letitia Hasser

Printed in the United States of America

To every girl who still believes in fairy tales.

Chapter 1

I WISH I HAD MAGICAL POWERS

LIBBY

I hear the front door open, then listen as my sister Mackenzie tries to be quiet when she enters our apartment. The loud squeak of the hinges causes her to fail miserably. I roll over in bed and look at the clock. It's early, not even five in the morning. I don't know where she stayed last night, but I do know it wasn't here. I also know that if I ask her where she was all night, she won't tell me. She never tells me anything anymore, which is annoying as hell and highly frustrating. There was a time when we shared everything with each other, a time when both my sisters, Mac and Fawn, shared everything with me. That all changed around Halloween, when Fawn started dating her boyfriend, Levi. I don't know *why* things changed then, but I know they *did*. I roll back over and close my eyes, ignoring her as she comes into the bedroom and fumbles around in the dark. I keep ignoring her as her bed squeaks as she gets into it. I hear her move around some more like she can't get comfortable.

"Lib, are you up?" she whispers into the dark. I hold back a sigh of frustration. I've always had a problem getting back to sleep once I'm awake.

"Maybe," I whisper back.

"Tony had a heart attack."

"What?" I sit up and flip on my lamp, blinking as my eyes adjust to the light.

"Tony had a heart attack," she repeats.

My heart sinks. Tony is the owner of Tony's Pizzeria, just a couple of blocks from our apartment. When I moved to New York City to go to school six years ago, Tony's Pizzeria was the first place that felt a little like home. The first time I walked into the shop, Tony welcomed me with open arms. Every time after that, he greeted me like he had known me my whole life, like I was a part of his family. He was always there with a warm smile and friendly hug.

Tony's has become the place I go when I need a moment to think or someone to talk to—that someone being Tony's wife, Martina, a woman I have come to care for deeply. She's always, but always, given me her time, her ear, and her advice. She and her husband are two of the kindest people I know. They remind me of my parents in a lot of ways. Tony has a warmth about him, and Martina is sweet to the bone and generous with advice. Even when advice is not exactly what you're looking for.

"When . . . ? Is . . . is he okay? Is Martina okay?"

"It was a few days ago. He's okay. He had surgery. Antonio said he'll be starting physical therapy soon. Martina is with him."

Of course she's with him. Martina is always at her husband's side; where he goes, she goes.

"Oh god," I whisper. "Who's running the shop?" If Tony just had a heart attack, he can't run it; Martina can't because she won't leave her husband's side. And Antonio? Well, Antonio, their only son, already has a full-time job as a firefighter—and he hates the pizzeria. I can't imagine him wanting to run the shop for his parents.

"Antonio's been taking care of things," she says.

I shake my head. Martina told me a while back, when I asked why Antonio didn't work at the shop, that Antonio resented the pizzeria, that he felt like the business was slowly killing his dad. I'm sure his father having a heart attack has only made him hate the place even more now.

"He's struggling, so I'm going to try and help out when I can." Her words pull me from my thoughts. I look over at her once more.

"I'll help, too," I say instantly. It might be awkward, though, since I've had a crush on Antonio for three years and he doesn't seem to like me much. Every time I've been around him, he's growled or glared at me for whatever reason. Personally, I think he is a jerk—a hot jerk, but a jerk all the same. Still, I adore his parents and wouldn't be able to look at myself in the mirror if I didn't at least try to help them out in some way while they are dealing with such a difficult situation.

"I know Martina will appreciate that," she says.

I notice that her eyes are tired and her face is red, like she's been crying. I want to ask her what's wrong, but I fight the urge, turn the light back off, and lie down. I'm not a heartless cow; I've tried talking to Mackenzie until I'm blue in the face, but no matter what I say or do, she refuses to open up to me. As the baby of the family, I'm used to people . . . well . . . babying me. Still, it's frustrating when it happens. I might be younger than my sisters, but I'm a grown woman who has the ability to think, give advice, and help out when needed. I wish they would see that.

Twenty minutes later, with sleep evading me and Mac snoring softly, I get out of bed and head for the bathroom to get ready for work. Once I'm out of the shower, I wrap myself in my robe and go through my morning routine. I recurl my dark-brown hair, pulling the top of it back away from my face with bobby pins and spraying enough hair spray to hold it throughout the day. Then I put on a full face of makeup, including a deep-red lipstick. I leave the bathroom quietly to get dressed in the living room, where I keep my wardrobe. Our apartment is tiny. The bedroom is just big enough for our twin beds, Mac's dresser, and our shared nightstand. The living room and small kitchen are separated by a wall with a cutout. Our couch sits under that opening, and our flat-screen TV hangs on the opposite wall, over a small black entertainment stand. My wardrobe is where the dining room table would be if we had one. Thank god we don't, and I say that because I have an obsession with buying clothes, bags, and shoes. As it is, my bed is hiked up off the floor so that I have room to store my seasonal clothing in three plastic totes beneath it. After rummaging through my stuff, I settle on a pair of navy-blue wool slacks with a wide leg and a high waist, and a navy silk blouse with white polka dots. I pair these with navy-blue Mary Janes that have a wide, three-inch stacked heel. After getting dressed, I make myself a bowl of Frosted Flakes that I eat while leaning against the counter and scrolling through my phone for a flower shop near my job. I finish my cereal, rinse my bowl, and wipe down the counters before grabbing my black wool trench coat, my Coach purse—a gift from my parents when I turned twenty-one—and my keys. Not in the mood to take the train, I catch a cab to work.

I let myself into the Madison Avenue salon a little before eight and lock the door behind me. Palo, the owner, won't be here for another hour or two, depending on his client schedule, and everyone else won't be in until closer to opening. Two months ago, Palo promoted me to assistant manager. It's my job to get things ready in the mornings, like starting the wax machines, making sure all the supplies are stocked, and letting in the cleaning crew.

Palo's is one of the top-rated salons in the city, not only because some of the most talented people in the industry work here but because the space screams luxury. Before you even enter the shop, you know you're going to get first-class service . . . just because of the Madison Avenue location. When you enter the salon, you see that the entire space is open, so clients can watch others get their hair or makeup done from one of the black leather couches in the front. We have one makeup station, which is mine, and six stylist stations. All the stations have white leather chairs in front of floating glass shelves and standing mirrors with black frames. There is no art on the walls, because who needs art when you're creating it? At least that's what Palo says. Personally, I would love to see some color around here.

I've worked at Palo's for three years. I started as an apprentice right after I graduated from Aveda, which is, in my opinion, one of the best cosmetology schools in the world. My goal was to do theatrical makeup on Broadway or for one of the morning shows that tape in New York City. But since starting at the salon, I haven't attempted to do either of those things; honestly, I don't know if makeup and hair is what I want to do forever. I used to think it was. I always assumed that because I loved makeup and hair, I would love being a stylist for a living. Now . . . I'm not so sure. I *like* my job. I'm really good at it, the money is great, and I've made some amazing friends along the way, but I don't feel fulfilled anymore. I feel like I'm missing something, only I'm too scared to figure out what that something is.

Shoving away that depressing realization, I walk across the black marble floors to the office, take off my coat, and stow my bag before clocking in and getting to work.

~

More than nine hours later, my feet are tired, my head is throbbing from inhaling hair products all day, and my stomach is grumbling from not having had time to eat lunch. I head into the hospital and try to focus on sending a text to my sister Fawn to let her know I'll see her later tonight. My sisters and I have plans to go to an art show in SoHo, where one of Fawn's friend's pieces will be on display. It's not something I'm really looking forward to after being on my feet all day, but I miss my sisters. It will be worth it to spend some time with them. I take the elevator up to the third floor, then follow the directions the lady at the front desk gave me. My shoes click-clack loudly, the sound bouncing off the walls with each and every step. Shifting my purse and the huge bouquet of lilies and roses I'm holding in my arms, I scan each room number until I finally reach the one I've been looking for. I shift the bouquet again, then reach for the handle of the door just as it begins to swing open. As I look over the top of the flowers, a familiar set of dark-brown eyes lock with mine. My heart starts to race.

"Princess."

Antonio's rough voice greets me with the annoying nickname he uses for me. He crowds my space, forcing me to shuffle back to avoid being pressed against him. (I *totally* don't want that.) Once I'm standing in the middle of the empty hall a few feet from him, he closes the door behind him. He crosses his arms over his chest and plants his boot-covered feet wide apart. Lowering the flowers so I can see him, I wish—not for the first time—that I had magical powers to make him seem grotesque. Unfortunately, I *don't* have those powers. He only seems to become more handsome each time I see him. His dark hair is lazily styled in a way that makes it look like he just ran his fingers through it, and his olive skin that's not even been kissed by the sun is a gift from the Italian blood flowing through his veins. He has cut cheekbones, a strong square jaw, full lips, and dark eyes surrounded by thick, dark lashes. Last but totally not least, there's his body—tall, lean, and powerful. I hate him . . . Or I really wish I could hate him.

"Dad can't have flowers," he states, moving his eyes from me to the bouquet I'm holding.

My stomach drops.

"Wh-what?"

"Can't have flowers. He just had surgery, so they don't want flowers in his room."

"Oh." I look from him to the flowers, feeling disappointed. I should have asked before I bought them. I just thought anyone staying in a cold, sterile hospital deserved to have flowers to look at. "I'll—"

He cuts me off. "I'll take them to the house."

My eyes go back to his, and I could swear I catch a flash of regret. I know I imagine it, though. He's never, not *ever*, nice to me. Why would he regret being mean now?

"Mom will enjoy looking at them when she's home."

He's right. His mom *will* enjoy them. She loves flowers, and I know this because even though their house doesn't have much green space, she plants flowers every spring in the hanging baskets outside their windows and in big pots on either side of her front door. She even has flowers outside the pizza shop in one of the big planters near the street, which on other blocks are normally collecting a fair amount of garbage from passersby.

"Thanks." I bite my lip as I hold out the flowers toward him. His eyes drop to my mouth and turn angry as he takes them. His angry looks really don't surprise me anymore. While I've been lusting over him, wishing I could hate him, he's been doing a really great job of hating *me*. I don't know what I did to make him dislike me as much as he does, but there is no denying he *totally* dislikes me.

"You gonna go in and visit?"

"Yes," I answer, but I don't move. I don't move because he looks tired, actually exhausted. I can see that he's trying to hold himself together and stay strong for his parents.

"Are you okay?" I ask softly, taking a step toward him. Without thinking, I rest my hand on his upper arm. His eyes drop to my hand, then shoot up to mine. Releasing him when I see the look in his eyes, I brace myself. Good thing I do, since the next words that come out of his mouth feel like a punch to the gut.

"My dad had a heart attack, he had surgery, he can't work, I gotta run the shop, and Mom's a mess. How do you *think* I'm doing?" he replies in a clipped tone.

I take a step back and pull in a deep breath so I don't do something stupid like cry in front of him.

"Why"—I pull in another breath through my nose, fighting back the sting of tears—"why are you always such a jerk to me?" I hold up my hand to cut him off when I see his mouth open. "Never mind. I don't care." I turn away from him, put my hand on the door handle, push down, and walk into the room without knocking. I close the door behind me.

When I step into the room, the sight that greets me makes my stomach twist. Tony is lying in the hospital bed asleep, looking pale and thin. Martina is sitting in a chair next to his bed, holding his hand, with her head bowed and her eyes closed.

Seeing Tony in that bed and Martina at his side, a different kind of pain slithers through my chest.

"*Cara.*"

Martina's voice startles me, and I focus on her.

"Hey." I step farther into the room and get close to her. I curve my hand around her shoulder, then bend at the waist to kiss her cheek.

"*Cara.*" She repeats the Italian word for "dear," and my eyes start to sting again. I can hear the pain in her voice.

"How are you holding up?" I ask, leaning back to look at her.

Her eyes close as she shakes her head. When she opens up her eyes again, she turns her head toward Tony, who's still asleep.

"Doctors say he's gonna be okay, so I'll be okay," she answers.

My heart twists again. There is no doubt that she loves her husband, and I know that she loves him in a way that if, god forbid, he were to pass, she would follow behind him. That's how strong their love is. I don't think either of them would survive without the other. No way.

"I would have come sooner, but Mackenzie just told me this morning," I say.

She lets out a long breath. Her eyes leave her husband and come back to me.

"I . . ." She takes a shaky breath, and tears fill her eyes. "I haven't thought much about anything since he told me his chest was hurting him and I forced him to come to the hospital. I'm sorry I didn't think to call."

"Please don't apologize," I whisper, watching her eyes close. A single tear slides down her pale cheek. "It will be okay." I take a seat in the empty chair next to her.

"I know, *cara*, I'm just worried not only about Tony but about Antonio. He's been running himself ragged working at the shop—and he's still going in to the firehouse. It's too much for one person. I don't know what to do."

"He'll be okay as long as you and Tony are okay," I assure her, taking her hand and squeezing it. "I rearranged my hours at the salon today so I can help out at the shop for a few hours in the evenings, and Mackenzie said she'll help out as well."

"You're a good girl." She covers my hand with her own, giving it a squeeze. "One day Antonio will open his eyes and see that, too."

Her statement doesn't surprise me. She's gotten it in her head that her son and I should be together. I used to tell her it'd never happen while secretly hoping it would. Now I don't secretly wish for anything having to do with her son.

"You look pretty today. Did you do anything fun?"

"Just work."

"You work too much."

This is spoken in a rough, low voice. My eyes fly to the bed. Tony's tired eyes are open and on me.

"Hey, you." I get up and walk around to the opposite side of the bed so I can lean over him and kiss his cheek. "How are you feeling?" I ask when I lean back.

He rolls his eyes. "I'm fine. Just wish everyone would stop worrying so much," he says.

I smile softly.

"He wants to get out of here," Martina says. My eyes go to her. "He keeps complaining to the doctors about how many tests they are running, how many drugs they are giving him, and how long he has to be here for." She shakes her head.

"I should be allowed to leave when I want," he grumbles.

"I think the doctors know what they're doing. Maybe you should listen to them," I suggest.

He presses his lips tightly together. "They want me to go to rehab at some fancy place upstate. I don't have time to do that. I have a business to run."

"You're going," Martina says firmly. Tony looks over at her. "If the doctors say you need to go, you're going. End of discussion." She slashes her hand in the air, and he sighs.

"A man should be allowed to make his own choices."

"How about you focus on getting well?" I say.

He looks at me. "I don't think I have a choice in the matter."

"I think you're right about that," I agree. I swallow down a bubble of laughter when he directs an annoyed glare at his wife.

Yes, Tony and Martina love each other—but lord do they bicker all the time.

Hearing a knock at the door, I turn my head. A man wearing dark-blue scrubs comes into the room, pushing a wheelchair. He greets everyone with a smile.

"I'm here to take you for your ultrasound, Mr. Moretti."

Tony grumbles, "Great, more tests." He looks back at me. "Thank you for coming to see us."

"Anytime." I kiss his cheek again, then walk over to Martina, who's now standing at the end of the bed.

Wrapping my arms around her, I give her a hug.

When I start to pull away, she tightens her hold on me and whispers in my ear, "Watch over Antonio for me."

I nod my head, then hug her tighter.

"I'll come visit again soon. You have my number. Let me know if you need anything."

"I will, *cara*." She kisses my cheek, then lets me go.

I take one more glance at them over my shoulder, giving them a wave before I leave the room. I wonder how hard it will be to keep my promise to Martina.

Chapter 2

Are You . . . Are You Being Nice to Me?

Libby

I stick my head into Palo's office and smile when his eyes meet mine. I watch his full lips tip up into a grin. Palo is a gorgeous Puerto Rican man with dark hair, caramel-colored skin, and brown eyes that look almost golden in the bright lights of the salon. He's one of the nicest men I've ever met—and beyond talented. He's been featured in tons of fashion magazines and newspapers for his work as a stylist. As young as he is—only thirty-three—he's made a name for himself with not only the who's who of Manhattan but with movie and Broadway stars alike. People book months in advance to have his magical hands in their hair.

"You off, love?" He swivels his chair around so he's closer to me.

"Yep. My last client just left," I tell him as I slip on my coat over a black button-up shirt with a frilly neckline and long, flowing sleeves that I wore over black skinny jeans and black pointy-toed booties with a slim three-inch heel.

"How's your sister's boyfriend doing?"

My fingers pause on the buttons of my coat. Two nights ago when I went out with Mackenzie and Fawn for the art show, Fawn's boyfriend, Levi—a police detective—was shot. Thankfully he's okay, but it was still very unnerving to see my sister worried out of her mind that she might lose the love of her life. I also learned earlier that evening the secret Mackenzie had been keeping from not only me but from everyone. She's been secretly seeing Levi's partner, Wesley. Mackenzie told us that they met at a bar just before Thanksgiving, when her actual date stood her up. They hooked up that night and then again a few days later; both times she made some assumptions about him and took off, thinking she'd never see him again. Then he showed up on Thanksgiving, having no idea that his partner's girlfriend was Mackenzie's sister. I guess after that, like they say, the rest is history. Now my family knows about them. Mom is, of course, over the moon that not only one but two of her daughters are actually dating living, breathing men who have the potential to put rings on their fingers and give her grandbabies to dote on.

"Hey."

I feel a hand on my arm, and I snap myself back into the present and blink at Palo.

"Sorry. Yes, he's okay. He's actually doing great," I murmur.

His head tips to the side, and his eyes scan my face as I finish up the buttons on my coat.

"Are you okay?"

"Yeah, just a little tired." Actually, I'm not really tired—even though I should be. All day I've felt as if I drank too much coffee; my whole body is wired with adrenaline and anxiety. Tonight I start helping out at Tony's Pizzeria—much to the dismay of Antonio, who wasn't very happy when I called to tell him I would be in this evening. Still, he didn't tell me *not* to come, which goes to show how badly he needs the help right now.

"You need to relax more," Palo chides gently.

I grab my bag from the drawer, then lean over to kiss his scruffy jaw.

"My next full day off, I'm not moving from the couch." This is not a lie. Whenever I have an entire day off, I spend it in sweats, on the couch, watching whatever scary movies I can find and eating nothing but junk food.

"Good. And I expect you out for drinks soon. I also have someone I want you to meet."

Oh lord.

"Palo . . . ," I sigh.

"It will be casual. Promise." He smiles, trying to cover his lie.

With Palo, nothing is ever casual. He's been trying forever to find a man for me.

"You are *not* setting me up again."

"Why not?" he asks, sounding offended.

I wonder if I sounded just like him when I tried to set up Fawn with someone and she told me no.

"Because—"

"*Because* is not an answer, love."

"It is!" I insist. "It's *my* answer. That's *because* the last time you set me up, the guy left me with a hundred-dollar tab at the bar. Or *because* the last time you set me up, the guy was old enough to be my father. Or *because* . . ."

"I get the point." He shakes his head and grabs my hand, his lips tipping up into an amused grin for a moment before his expression turns serious. "You're a beautiful woman, Libby. You're young. You should be dating."

I agree. I *should* be dating, but every single time I've gone out with a man in this city, it's ended badly. The men I've dated either expect me to be really stupid or really easy, and I'm neither of those things. I might not know what I want to do with the rest of my life, but I do know that I want to be successful. I want to be more than just a pretty object on the arm of a man, and I don't want to have casual sex with random men until I find The One. I want to share my body with someone I care about, and who cares about me. I simply have yet to find a guy who meets my criteria.

"I'll see you tomorrow," I tell him, needing this conversation to end.

"You're off tomorrow," he reminds me.

I roll my eyes. I totally forgot. Tomorrow *is* my day off.

"Right. I forgot, since tomorrow I'll spend most of the day running dresses all over the city."

He knows all about my side business. Two years ago, I was doing a home visit for one of my very wealthy clients who was attending a charity ball later that evening. She showed me all her designer gowns and dresses—she only ever wore them once. All I could think was that it was such a waste. No way should Michael Kors, Vera Wang, Tom Ford, or Phillip Lim be forgotten in someone's closet. That's when I came up with my business idea. I talked to her and a few of my other clients. Surprisingly, it didn't take me much time to convince them to go along. Once I got them to agree, I got pictures of their dresses and accessories that they wouldn't mind lending out. That's how I started Designer Closet. I rent out items from other people's closets. Clients will tell me what they're looking for, and I'll find it. They pay a set price; then they return the item or items to me when they're done with them. I have the items cleaned before I return them to their owners. I haven't made millions from the business, but I have made a decent amount of money. Enough that I'll be able to put a sizable down payment on a condo in the city.

"Make sure you also spend some time resting."

"I will. I'll see you the day after." I kiss Palo's cheek once more before I leave him in the office. Walking through the salon, I smile at the other stylists, but I don't stop to talk since they all have clients.

"See ya, Libby," calls Max, our receptionist. He's prettier than most women I know. I turn to find him leaning against the receptionist desk with a smile on his face. His full lips are glossy, and his eyes are lined with dark pencil, making them stand out against his pale complexion.

"See you, Max. Have a good night." I smile back, then turn and open the door.

As I step outside into the cold, I shiver. I stop and pull my hat and gloves from my purse, putting on both before heading down the block. As much as I want to take a cab across town, I don't. Right now, traffic is ridiculous; everyone is trying to get home. Going to the subway station on the corner, I take the stairs down to the packed platform. Two trains pass before I'm finally able to get on one. By the time I make it to my side of town, it's five thirty—thirty minutes later than I told Antonio I would be at Tony's. I don't go home to change since I don't have time; I just head right to the shop. I step inside Tony's and pull in a lungful of warm air. It smells like pizza dough and comfort. Peggy is at the front counter taking orders, and an overwhelmed-looking Hector and Marco are making pizzas. I hurry through the crowd of people waiting in line to place their orders and go to the office. I don't knock. I walk in, then stop in my tracks when I see Antonio's shirtless, muscular back. My stomach twists and dips at the sight before he pulls a plain navy-blue T-shirt down over his head.

"Uh . . . hey." I clear my throat and avoid his eyes as I tuck away my purse in the corner of the room, then take off my coat and put it over my bag.

"You can't wear that shirt out there," he says.

Since I'm the only person in the room, I know he's talking to me. I turn to look at him.

"Here." He holds out a T-shirt the same color as his, with TONY'S written in yellow on the front. "You're not going to argue with me?" He raises a brow, seeming surprised.

"This shirt cost close to two hundred dollars," I say as an answer, watching his jaw clench.

"Right. See you out front." He leaves without looking at me again. Watching the door close, I shake my head. I don't know what the hell his problem is, but I do know that he needs to get over it.

Changing into the T-shirt he gave me, I tie a knot in the waist at the side since it's too long to leave loose or tuck in. Once I'm ready, I leave the office and head through the half door that cuts off the back of the shop from the front.

"Where do you want me?" I ask Antonio.

He's kneading large balls of pizza dough on a flat stainless-steel surface that's covered with flour.

"What do you know how to do?" he asks without even glancing at me.

"Everything," I say.

His doubt-filled eyes move to me. He scans me from head to toe, and I fight the urge to fidget. I'm not lying. When I turned sixteen, I wanted money to buy all the makeup and clothes my mom wouldn't buy for me, so I got a job at a pizza shop down the street from my parents' house on Long Island. I worked there until I graduated from high school. I loved that job, and I was so good at it that the owners offered me a full-time manager's slot if I decided to stay local for college.

"All right, you can help me make pies," Antonio finally says.

I nod, go to the sink and wash my hands, then stand next to him. We all work in sync, and I'm side by side with Antonio. He presses out the balls of dough into round crusts with his hands, I take them from him and add the toppings, and Hector and Marco put the pizzas in the stone oven and then in boxes when they're done. At about eight o'clock, the line inside dies down, and the phone stops ringing every five minutes with people placing orders. I'm finally able to breathe a bit.

"I don't know how you're wearing those shoes right now," Peggy states as I pass Hector another pizza to put in the oven.

Turning to face her, I smile and lift the three-inch heel of my shoe off the ground to inspect it.

"I've been walking in heels since I was four, when I convinced my mom to buy me a pair of the plastic ones from the grocery store," I tell her with what I know is a nostalgic smile on my face. "I wore them everywhere. When I finally wore them out, I made my mom crazy by begging her every day to buy me a real pair. She didn't give in until I was thirteen, but once the seal was broken, I never wore regular shoes again."

"Sheesh," Peggy mutters. "I'm forty-two, and I've only worn heels twice in my life." She holds up two fingers. "Once when I got married to Hector"—she lifts her chin Hector's way—"and when our daughter was baptized. My feet still hurt remembering what it felt like wearing those darn shoes around."

Hector is Mexican American and is still handsome at forty-three. He's short, with black hair that's started to gray at his temples and a black goatee that I bet he dyes to keep it from going gray like his hair. He's sweet, and he and Peggy make a cute couple. She has dark reddish-brown hair, pale skin, and a petite figure. I bet their daughter is beautiful. I do know that she's smart—she just started high school this year at a private school in the Bronx, which is why Peggy started working here part-time. Their daughter got a full ride, but she still needs money for extracurricular activities, which at a private school are not cheap.

"I guess I'm just used to them." I shrug.

"You really shouldn't be wearing heels back here in the kitchen," Antonio says, breaking into our conversation. When I turn to look at him, I notice a frown on his face. "They are a health hazard," he states.

I grit my teeth.

"I like the heels," Marco says, a cheeky smile on his handsome face. "I like them *a lot*." He winks, and I roll my eyes. He flirts with every woman who comes into the shop.

"Marco . . . ," Antonio growls.

Marco shrugs his broad shoulders. Marco's half Italian, half African American. He's close to forty but looks around thirty-five. He's a little taller than I am in heels, with dark hair, greenish-brown eyes, and a killer smile that gets him tons of attention from the women who come in. He's also very married to a woman named Lola who is okay with her husband flirting because she knows he will never step out on her—if he ever did stray, her three older brothers would kill him.

"I personally don't care *what* kind of shoes you wear, *chiquita*," Hector breaks in, patting my shoulder. "You're fast, you didn't crack under pressure, and every order was made correctly. In my opinion, you can wear whatever kind of shoes you want."

"You kicked ass tonight, girl. Tony and Martina would be proud," Marco says.

I let their words settle deep inside me. Hector and Marco have both worked here since before I started coming here, years ago. Tony has trusted them with the shop more than once, so it makes me feel good that they think I've done a good job tonight.

"Thanks, guys," I say softly.

"You wanna put toppings on these pies, Princess, or do you want to continue chatting?" Antonio asks.

I turn back to the counter behind me and find that I'm behind by three pies. I don't answer him; I just get back to work. I wonder if I should ask my sisters' boyfriends if they would investigate me if Antonio suddenly turned up missing. Seriously. One day, I might just kill him.

◆

"I can finish that up for you," Antonio says three hours later.

I lift my eyes from the table I'm wiping down to look at him.

"I got it." I go back to wiping and yawn; the adrenaline I felt earlier today is long gone, and exhaustion has firmly taken its place.

"You're tired. Go rest in the office until I finish up; then I'll walk you home," he says as he walks across the now-closed shop toward me. Marco and Hector both left about an hour ago because they will both be coming back around eleven in the morning to open up and get things ready for lunch. Peggy left when her husband did, after cleaning up the kitchen and putting things away. I decided to stay since I can sleep in tomorrow morning before I have to start running dresses around the city.

"I'm almost done, and I don't need you to walk me home." I move to another table, wipe down the chairs and the top of the table, and straighten the shakers and the napkin holder.

"And *I* can finish up," he tells me, trying to take the rag from my grasp. I pull it from his hold with a hard tug.

"Yeah, and so can *I*." I glare at him before moving around him to another table.

"I'm trying to be nice to you."

"Nice? You're *never* nice to me. Just so you know, if you *are* trying to be nice, you could do it by just saying thank you."

"I didn't ask you to come."

Seriously?

I wonder how much time you get for committing murder if you've actually spent time plotting someone's death beforehand.

"You're right. You *didn't* ask for my help," I agree. "But I'm here because I like this place and I love your parents." I lock eyes with his and tip my head to the side. "Why are you so miserable all the time?"

"I'm not." He crosses his arms over his chest.

I try not to notice how his muscles flex or how his shirt gets snug against his pecs and abs when they do.

Annoyed with myself for finding him attractive when he's such a jerk, I shake my head. "You are."

"I'm *not* miserable." He scowls.

I roll my eyes and move to another table. "Sure you're not." I let out a sarcastic laugh. "Even now, you're scowling." I look down and start cleaning another table.

"I don't scowl," he denies.

I look up at him and roll my eyes again when I see that he is indeed still scowling.

"Sure you don't."

"I don't."

"Whatever. This conversation is completely pointless," I say, looking away from him. "Don't you have something to do?"

I look up when he doesn't leave. When my eyes meet his, the air around us seems to shift. I see something in his gaze that makes my stomach muscles clench and unclench.

I don't know how long we stare at each other, but it feels like forever before he clears his throat and finally looks away.

"I'm gonna finish shutting everything down."

"Right."

I watch him go, wondering what the hell that was about. I finish cleaning the tables, then do a quick sweep of the floors. Around eleven, I walk back to the office. A few seconds later, he comes in behind me. Deciding not to bother with changing back into the shirt I wore here, I fold it neatly and put it in my purse. Then I put on my coat, hat, and gloves. When I turn around, I see he's put on a black down jacket and a beanie. I don't *want* to think he looks good wearing a beanie, but he does. It makes his already-strong cheekbones seem stronger, his eyes seem darker, and him seem overall more mysterious. Pushing those stupid thoughts away, I leave him in the office and head for the front door.

As I walk away, I hear him coming up behind me.

"Have a good night," I murmur without looking back.

I stop when I feel his hand wrap around my wrist, between my coat sleeve and glove. A shot of what can only be described as electricity shoots through my system at his touch, charging every cell in my body. It startles me.

"I'm gonna walk you home," he says.

I turn to look up at him. "I'm fine walking alone." I attempt to pull away from his grasp, but his fingers only seem to tighten.

"I'm gonna walk you home," he repeats more firmly.

I fight back a sigh of frustration. If he wasn't such a jerk, I would think his worrying about me making it home safely was sweet. Unfortunately, he's proved to be mostly a jerk.

"I'm really okay to walk alone. It's not even two blocks," I say, trying once more to tug my wrist from his fingers.

He doesn't let me go or reply. Instead, he opens the door, shuffles me outside, then shuts and locks it. Scooting me farther to the side, he uses his key to open a metal box there, puts the key in, and turns the dial on it. The metal shutters that cover the glass windows slide down.

"Now, like I said, I'm walking you home," he tells me once he's locked the box back up.

I barely resist the urge to kick him in the shin. He finally releases his hold on my wrist, and I grit my teeth as I turn away from him and head for my block. I try not to look like I'm stomping, but that's exactly what I'm doing. When I finally reach my place, I head up the steps and open the front door to the town house.

"Thanks for all your help tonight, Libby," he says.

I turn around, knowing my mouth is probably hanging open.

"I appreciate it, and I know Mom and Dad appreciate it, too. You really did do an awesome job."

"Are you . . . are you being *nice* to me?" I point at myself.

I swear I see his lips twitch, but I know it has to be a figment of my imagination—just like I must have imagined him thanking me.

"Go on in." He lifts his chin to indicate the door behind me. "Flicker the lights once you're upstairs so I know you're good."

"Flicker the lights . . . ?" I repeat, feeling my stomach warm.

"Yeah."

"I'm good. You can go."

"Lib, go in and flick the lights," he repeats, sounding like a jerk once again.

I sigh.

"That didn't last long," I mutter under my breath as I turn on my heel and head inside.

I swear I hear him chuckle as I shut the door behind me. I figure it won't kill him to wait a few minutes, so I stop and collect all the mail.

I shove it under my arm before I head up to the second floor and use my key to enter the apartment.

Without knowing exactly why I do it, I leave the light off and walk across the apartment to look out the window. I wonder if Antonio actually cares enough to have waited to see that I've gotten in okay. When I peek out and see him standing on the sidewalk, looking up at the windows to my apartment, my stomach drops. I rush quickly back across the room, almost falling on my face to get to the light switch. After flickering the lights, I head back to the window and peek out again. I watch him walk down the sidewalk with his hands tucked into the pockets of his jacket. I shake my head, not sure how to deal with the fact that I now know he has the ability to be sweet.

Chapter 3

MOSTLY A JERK

LIBBY

I'm lying on my couch in a pair of old, ratty cutoff sweats, a tank top, and a baggy man's flannel shirt. My hair is in a bun on top of my head. There's a half-empty carton of lo mein on the coffee table in front of me, along with an open bag of chips and the candy from the Christmas stocking my mom gave me. I stare at the TV, watching a woman attempt to get away from a ghost—the same ghost that has tried to kill her at least three times since the movie started.

"Don't go in there," I whisper to the TV as the woman puts her hand on the door handle of the room the ghost is currently in.

I'm so engrossed in the movie that I jump when someone knocks on my apartment door. I sit up quickly, causing tiny, empty, silver chocolate wrappers to fly out around me. Looking at the door, my heart races.

"Libby?"

Hearing Antonio's familiar voice, I stare at the door in disbelief.

"Libby?" he calls as I get up off the couch.

I glance at the clock to see that it's just after eight o'clock. I got home from my parents' house on Long Island this morning after spending Christmas and a few days with them. It was nice to get away, but I'm happy to be home.

I look out the peephole when I get to the door. Sure enough, Antonio is standing on the other side. Shaking my head, I unlock the dead bolt and pull open the door.

"Antonio, wh—"

"I've been calling you." He cuts me off as he pushes his way into my apartment.

"What?" My eyes go from the hallway to him.

"I've called you at least a dozen times, if not more," he says.

I blink at him.

"What . . . ? Why?"

"You need to work tonight."

"Pardon?" I hiss, not saying what I really want to say. That would be that I don't actually *work* at Tony's, and that if I go in to help out, I do it as a favor to his parents and him. Yes, I might be getting paid for the time I'm there, but I still don't officially work at the pizzeria.

"They need me at the station. One of the guys called in, so they're down a man. This normally wouldn't be a big deal, but Marco's off tonight, Peggy just went home to be with Valeria, and Hector can't close the shop alone."

"So you need my help?"

"Yes."

"You could have just asked nicely," I tell him.

He shoves his hands into the front pockets of his jeans, looking uncomfortable.

"Can you please help me out?"

"Yes."

"Really?" he asks, surprised.

"Yes." I roll my eyes, then head for my closet. "I just need to get ready."

"I'll wait and walk with you."

"I can find my own way after I finish getting ready," I point out. "Don't you need to head to the station?"

"I'll wait," he repeats, going over to my couch and taking a seat.

Trying to ignore the fact that there's an extremely handsome man in my apartment, I grab a pair of jeans from my wardrobe, along with the T-shirt he gave me with the Tony's logo on the front. I take everything with me into my bedroom and shut the door. I change quickly, then head into the bathroom to brush my teeth and my hair. Once I'm done, I go back into the living room and grab a pair of socks out of my drawer. I pick up my boots, then take a seat on the couch next to him to put them on.

"This is a lot of junk food . . . ," he says, sounding slightly horrified.

I notice that he's picked up all the wrappers from the candy I've eaten tonight and wadded them into a ball in his hand.

"No, it's not," I lie, looking at him.

His head tips to the side.

"I've never seen you without makeup," he says suddenly.

I expect him to add something that will make me want to kick him, so I brace myself.

"You don't need it."

Okay, I didn't expect him to say that.

Hearing a scream come from the TV, we both look at it.

"Scary movie?"

"Yes." I grab the remote and flip off the television, then pick up my half-eaten container of lo mein and put it away in the fridge so I can eat it later.

"You don't seem like the kind of girl who watches scary movies alone," he states as he stands up from the couch and watches me put on my coat, hat, and gloves.

"And exactly what kind of movies would you think I might watch?"

"Ones with lots of romance," he answers.

My nose scrunches up in disgust. "I hate romance movies. They are always so cliché. Guy and girl meet, guy is a jerk, girl is an idiot for him even when he's a jerk. Still, the girl always falls in love with him, forgetting that he was a jerk to begin with, and in the end that comes back to bite her in the ass when he's an even bigger jerk. She cries, usually a lot. He realizes at some point what he lost and then finally he begs her for forgiveness. Always—but *always*—she takes him back, even when she shouldn't."

"You really *don't* like romance movies." His lips twitch, and I roll my eyes again. "I'm learning a lot about you tonight, Princess." He chuckles, and I glare at him.

"Don't annoy me, Antonio."

I open the door to my apartment and sweep my hand outward, indicating he should leave ahead of me.

"Even annoyed, you're still pretty," he says, stopping to look down at me.

My stomach dips, then knots in a way that it never has before.

"Definitely pretty," he mutters as he walks out the door.

With a shake of my head, I step out after him and lock up behind me. Following him down to the first floor, my stomach still in knots, I stare at his back. I wonder what the hell is going on with him. When we reach the sidewalk, we walk side by side—so close that our arms brush.

"Here." He hands me a key, and I take it. "Hector's going to stay with you tonight, but he doesn't have his key with him. So you'll have to use mine. In the morning, I'll pick it up from you."

"I have work tomorrow."

"What time?"

"I have to leave by seven thirty."

"I'll be by before that."

Figuring it's pointless to argue about this, I sigh. "Okay."

"I'll have my cell on if you need anything," he says as we stop outside the door to Tony's.

I look up at him when he dips his head down toward me.

"It will be okay," I say quietly, seeing that he looks worried.

"I know it will." His eyes scan my face, making me shift uncomfortably. "Call me when you get home tonight."

"I'm not going to call you," I mutter.

His lips twitch into a smile before he shakes his head and walks away down the sidewalk.

"You coming in, *chiquita*?" Hector asks, startling me.

I spin around to face him, feeling my cheeks get warm at the knowledge that I was just standing on the sidewalk like an idiot female lead in a romance movie watching the jerk she's lusting after walk away.

"Come on." Hector tugs my hand and drags me inside.

I follow him in, drop my stuff in the office, and get to work.

∼

Hearing my cell phone ring, I reach out with my eyes still closed and pat the top of my bedside table until my hand lands on it. Picking it up, I squint one eye open, slide my finger across the screen, and then put it to my ear.

"Yeah?" I answer, half-asleep.

"You didn't call," Antonio says, his voice sounding rough. Like he just woke up.

"I told you I *wasn't* going to call."

"You get home okay?" he asks, ignoring my comment.

I sigh. "Yes . . ."

"Everything go okay tonight?"

"Yes."

"All right, babe. Go back to sleep."

He hangs up, and I pull my phone from my ear and stare at it.

"Babe? Now what the hell is that about?" I whisper my question into the dark, but of course get no answer in return. I drop my cell back to my bedside table, but it takes me forever to get back to sleep. The replay of Antonio's deep voice calling me "babe" is on a continuous loop in my mind.

∼

Hearing a knock on my apartment door early the next morning, I rush across to it, tying my robe as I go. I lift up on my tiptoes to check the peephole, then feel my heart start to beat a funny rhythm in my chest when I see Antonio standing outside. His head is turned to the left and tipped down like he's looking at something. Glancing at myself in the mirror hanging next to the door, I cringe. My hair is a mess because I went to bed last night with it wet. There are bags under my eyes from not sleeping much. I look toward my bedroom, wondering in vain if I have time to put on some under-eye concealer or brush my hair.

"Libby?" he calls through the door, knocking again.

I jump. With no other choice, I open the door a crack and look out.

"Hey . . . ," I say, hating myself a little for sounding as breathy as I do.

"Libby Reed, what is that man doing coming to see you this time of the morning?"

I wince, then poke my head out the door and look down the stairs. It's Miss Ina, the old woman who lives on the first floor. She's standing at the bottom of the steps dressed in a robe, her white hair flat on one side like she just woke up.

"Miss Ina, it's okay. It's just Antonio. You can go back to bed."

"Go back to bed?" She plants her hands on her hips, and I sigh.

Until a few days ago, I'd never shared more than a handful of words with the woman—honestly, she scared the crap out of me. Then Mac befriended her and invited her to our parents' house for Christmas dinner. It was during the drive to Long Island that I learned she's actually kind of nice in a grumpy-old-woman sort of way. I'm also starting to figure out that she's nosy. Okay, I already knew that she was nosy, but now that we've started to talk, she's become even *more* nosy.

"I can't go back to bed now that I know you're going to be alone in your apartment with a man while you're wearing nothing but a dressing gown."

"Miss Ina, he's just picking up a key. My virtue is safe," I mutter.

Her eyes go to Antonio and narrow.

I peek up at him to see him fighting back a smile.

"This isn't funny."

"It's a little funny, Princess," he says, looking at me.

Rolling my eyes, I look down the stairs at Miss Ina. "He's not even coming inside. You can go back to bed."

"Fine, but I'll be calling your mother about this later," she says.

I don't reply, just watch her hobble away with her walker.

Once she's out of sight, I look at Antonio. "I'll be right back." I leave the door open a crack and go to my bedroom. I find his key in the jeans I had on last night. I grab it and head back to the living room, then stop dead when I find Antonio in my kitchen and the door to the fridge open.

"What are you doing?"

"I didn't have a chance to have breakfast," he tells me.

I blink at him.

"You didn't have breakfast?"

"It's only six. Nothing was open." He shrugs, then looks into the fridge once more.

"Okay . . . so pick something up when you leave," I suggest.

His eyes move back to me. "Why? I'm here now."

"Antonio—"

"Have you eaten yet?" he asks, cutting me off.

I feel my head twitch. "No . . ."

"So I'll make us breakfast while you get ready for work," he states.

I stare at him, wondering if he's been abducted by aliens. First he tells me I'm pretty, then calls me "babe," and now he's offering to make me breakfast?

"Babe, you might want to get a move on. You need to get ready to leave," he says.

I look from him to the clock, then feel my eyes widen when I see that he's right. I don't have a lot of time before I need to leave for work. It's going to take me forever to sort out my hair. With no time to deal with whatever is going on with him, I drop his key to the restaurant in the kitchen and grab an outfit from my wardrobe. I go into my bedroom and shut the door behind me. On autopilot, I shower, do my hair and makeup, and get dressed. I've chosen a pair of black slacks and a black scoop-neck sweater with a bow that ties behind my neck—its cream ribbon matches my boots. When I'm done, I open the bedroom door and find that Antonio is no longer in the kitchen. He's sitting on my couch with two plates of scrambled eggs and toast in front of him on the coffee table, along with two cups of coffee.

"You gonna stare at it, or are you going to eat it?"

At his words, I meet his gaze, head across the room, and take a seat.

"Thank you," I mumble, picking up my plate.

"You have nothing but junk food in your fridge. How the hell do you have that body?" he asks as I take a bite of toast.

I almost choke on it when I try to swallow.

"I've always been skinny. I have healthy food, too . . ."

"Where?" he counters.

I look at him and narrow my eyes. "There's some canned veggies in the cupboard, and you found the eggs," I point out.

"Right . . . canned veggies and eggs." His lips twitch, and my stomach does that weird dip thing it's been doing a lot lately.

"I work a lot. I don't have time to cook three-course meals all the time, so I normally eat on the go," I say by way of self-defense as I grab the remote and turn on the TV. I flip around to find a morning news show.

"Do you make good money doing makeup and hair?"

Even though the question is asked casually, it still makes me feel a little strange—like there is a deeper question hidden behind it.

"Can I ask you why you're asking me that?"

"You told me the other day that the top you had on cost you two hundred dollars. I'm just curious if you bought it yourself or if someone got it for you."

"If *someone* got it for me?" I repeat.

His eyes wander over me in a way I try to tell myself I don't like all that much.

"Yeah. Did a man take you shopping, or did you buy it for yourself?"

"A man bought it for me," I toss back at him, enjoying watching his eyes shutter and his jaw clench. "That man was *my dad*. It was my birthday gift last year from him," I state, completely offended.

Suddenly I realize *exactly* what kind of girl he thinks I am. Dropping my half-eaten piece of toast on my plate and picking up my cup of coffee, I take both to the kitchen and drop them into the sink. I don't even bother to scrape the eggs off into the garbage.

"Libby . . . ," he calls, but I don't look at him.

"If you're done, I need to get to work." I grab my coat off the arm of the couch and put it on, along with my scarf. Then I pick up my purse.

"I didn't mean anything by my question."

"You did," I state, finally looking at him.

He flinches.

Whatever.

"I need to leave. Are you done?" I ask, seeing that he hasn't moved from his spot on the couch.

"Lib—"

"Fine. Just lock up before you go." I cut him off as I open the door and step out. I don't slam the door behind me even though I want to, but I do stomp down the stairs.

"I thought he wasn't going inside," Miss Ina says, startling me.

I jump in place, grabbing my chest.

"Miss Ina, not now. Please."

"I know, I know." She waves a hand at me. "You don't have time to talk because you need to get to work, but I expect you over for tea so we can talk about why you look ready to commit murder."

"How do you feel about helping me hide a body?"

"I'm old, girl, but I still have a life to live. I can't go to prison."

"Right," I sigh, defeated. My eyes widen when I hear my apartment door open and shut. "Crap," I whisper.

I rush to Miss Ina and shuffle her back into her apartment. I follow her and close the door as quietly as I can while she asks loudly, "What on earth are you doing?"

Putting my finger to my mouth in a silent demand, I then get up on my toes to look through her peephole until I see Antonio walk past her door. Letting out a relieved breath, my shoulders sag.

"Seems you got it bad for that boy," she murmurs.

I glare at her. "I hate him."

"I bet you do."

"No, seriously. I do. I hate him."

"Okay." Her lips twitch, and I fight the urge to stomp my foot to emphasize my point. "Is he gone?" she asks.

"Yes."

"Well, then, what are you doing? Don't you need to get to work?"

"What if he's outside?"

"If he's outside, then you know he's got it bad for you, too," she tells me.

"He hates me more than I hate him."

"Sure he does," she mutters, moving me out of the way and opening the door. "Now, go on."

"Why did Mac insist on befriending you?" I question.

Her nose scrunches up. "I don't know, but you need to go. I have things to do."

"Fine." I swallow, then peek out into the corridor. Seeing it empty, I step out and turn back to say thanks to her for letting me hide out in her apartment. Before I can, she slams the door and locks me out. "Grumpy old woman."

"I heard that!" she shouts.

I mouth "I heard that," then turn on my heel and open the front door to the house. Seeing Antonio standing on the sidewalk, I grit my teeth.

"Libby!" he calls, but I ignore him as I head to the edge of the sidewalk to catch a cab to work. "I'm sorry."

"Good."

"I shouldn't have asked you that."

"No, you shouldn't have," I agree, feeling him get close to where I'm standing.

"Can you look at me?"

"Don't you need to be somewhere?" I snarl, pissed at him and at myself.

I'm angry at myself for liking him when I shouldn't and angry at him for being a jerk one minute and sweet the next.

"Yes, but first I need to know that you forgive me for being a dick."

"I forgive you," I say immediately, hoping that will make him go away.

My eyes fly up to meet his when his fingers wrap around my chin.

"I'm really sorry," he repeats.

I swallow over the sudden lump that has formed in my throat.

"Okay."

"Do you forgive me?"

Looking into his eyes and seeing regret there, I pull in a deep breath and let it out while nodding.

"Can I hear you say it?" he asks softly.

"I forgive you," I whisper.

His fingers touch my jaw while his thumb sweeps across my bottom lip so lightly that I wonder if I imagine it. He steps back.

"Have a good day at work, Princess." He steps into the road and raises an arm. A cab pulls up and parks at the curb. He opens the door for me, and I slide into the back seat without looking at him again as he slams the door behind me.

"Where to?" the cab driver asks.

I give him the address to the salon as I turn to look over my shoulder at Antonio. He's standing with his hands tucked into the front pockets of his jeans, his eyes on my cab.

Do you have plans tomorrow night?

Looking at the text from Palo as I stand in the office at Tony's, I wonder exactly how I should answer his question. There are times he will have a client come in and ask if someone can do their hair or makeup for an event. So it could be that, but it could also be something else.

Maybe . . .

I type back and press "Send."

I'm taking that as a no, which means you're going out on a date tomorrow night. I think I met the perfect guy for you.

Fricking great.

Palo, do I really need to remind you of the last five dates you've set me up on?

No, and this guy is different.

How is he different?

He's young, he has manners, and he's RICH.

I sigh out loud as I type.

I don't care about money, Palo.

Every woman cares about money, Libby.

He's wrong. *I* don't care about money. I never have. Yes, I like nice things like most women do, but I don't need them. My parents were not rolling in it when I was growing up, but we were always happy. I grew up in a house full of laughter and love, which I know is way more important than material things.

Palo . . .

I leave just his name, thinking that says it all. It really does.

Please? For me? Just this one last time. If it doesn't work out, I won't ever set you up again.

Yeah, right. Like I believe that for one second.

Gahhhh! Fine.

I drop my cell phone into my purse, then turn and leave the office.

"What's going on with you?" Peggy asks as soon as she sees me. I wonder if it's that obvious that I'm annoyed.

"I have a date tomorrow night," I tell her, sounding as annoyed as I feel about the idea.

She looks at me, then looks over my shoulder. I watch a knowing smile form on her lips. Wondering what that's about, I look behind me. My lungs freeze when I realize that Antonio is standing close enough that he probably heard me say I have a date.

"A date! That's nice. Who is the guy?" Peggy questions.

I look at her, wishing the ground would fall out from under me and swallow me whole.

"I . . . I . . . don't know. It's a blind date."

"Oh, those are always fun. The mystery, the excitement . . . ," she says wistfully.

Yes, I really wish the ground would swallow me whole.

"Anyway"—she claps her hands so loud that I almost jump out of my skin—"time to get back to work."

"Right," I whisper before I scurry though the half door into the back of the shop, then through the swinging door into the kitchen.

I need to get away from everyone. I start to busy myself with washing the overly large metal bowls, utensils, and pots that are all sitting in the sink. Since the pot is almost as big as I am, I leave it for last. I turn to look over my shoulder when I hear Antonio's deep laughter behind me.

I can see him though the small crack in the door that leads to the front of the shop, standing at the counter. I watch a cute woman with short blonde hair lean across the counter toward him. My stomach drops, then sinks even lower when I see her grab a pen from the jar next to the register, take his hand, and write down what I'm guessing is her number on his open palm.

Turning away, I grit my teeth. It should not bother me that he just got a woman's number. It shouldn't bother me at all—but it still does. Finished with all the other dishes, I drop the pot in the sink and scrub it hard, until my arm hurts. I pull in one deep breath after another, trying to get my confused emotions under control. I wish I didn't have a crush on Antonio, that I could hate him like I say I do. I wish I didn't have to see his handsome face, didn't have to hear his deep voice, and I especially wish I didn't have to see him flirting with women. Okay, so I haven't really seen *him* flirt with women, but I have definitely seen *women* flirt with him, which is just as annoying.

"What did you do for Christmas?" Peggy breaks into my thoughts.

I pull my eyes off the pot I'm scrubbing and look at her.

"I went to Long Island to spend time with my parents for a couple days. What about you?" I ask, trying to sound casual.

"Hector has a huge family, and they all came over to the house for dinner on Christmas Eve. Then, on Christmas Day, we all went to his parents' house, opened gifts, and the kids and the guys all went to the park to play football while the wives cooked."

"That sounds like fun." I smile at her.

"It was." She smiles back, wiping down counters that don't really need to be wiped down. "I was an only child. Hector has three brothers and six sisters, so it's always loud and crazy, but it's nice."

"It sounds nice," I say.

Her eyes study me for a long time—so long that I start to feel awkward.

"Don't let it get to you, honey," she says softly. My heart thumps hard. "That was just his reaction to learning you have a date."

"What?" I breathe.

She gets close to me and drops her voice.

"Men are sometimes complete idiots. Men see something they want, but they don't go after it because they think it will always be there waiting for them until they're finally ready to make a move. You just showed Antonio that you're not waiting," she says, freaking me the heck out.

"I think—" I start to tell her that she's got it all wrong, but she doesn't let me finish.

"Don't." She shakes her head. "You can lie to yourself all you want, but I see it. I see it when he looks at you. I see it when you look at him. One day one of you is going to break, and I imagine that day is going to be soon. He did *not* like hearing that you have plans with another man. I don't know what his holdup is, but I imagine it has something to do with the woman that came before you."

Okay, I was freaked out before, but now I'm *totally* freaked out.

Is she right? Does Antonio like me? Am I that transparent when it comes to my feelings for him?

"Go on your date. Have fun, flirt, and pray to god that that boy finally pulls his head out of his ass like his mama has been telling him to do for years now."

Oh my god.

"Peggy, I hate to tell you this. As much as I love Martina and hate killing her dream, you both have to know that he can barely stand me. I actually think he might even *hate* me," I tell her.

She starts laughing so hard she doubles over from the effort.

I stare at her. "This isn't funny."

"It is." She sobers up and grabs hold of my arm. "Honey, that boy does *not* hate you."

"He does."

"He might wish he could, but he does *not* hate you any more than I hate ice cream with chocolate syrup, rainy days at home with my family, sunsets at the beach, and the man I love giving me everything I want."

Heart pounding hard, I beg for oxygen to fill my lungs. The idea that she could be right is almost too much for me to handle.

"It will be okay. You just pulled the veil off, and he's seeing clearly now. Sometimes men need a wake-up call. I think you just gave him his."

"He's a jerk, Peggy . . . ," I tell her while reminding myself of that fact.

Okay, so he can be sweet on occasion . . . but for the most part, he's been nothing but a jerk to me.

"I can see why you'd think that."

I don't think that—I know it, I think but don't say.

"I can't wait to see how this plays out. I've been reading romance novels for a long time. It will be nice to see a real-life one play out right in front of my eyes."

Blinking at her, I wonder if she's crazy. Actually, I don't wonder—I *know* she must be.

"Now stop hiding in here. I need you out front with me. There's too much testosterone in this place, and I don't like being outnumbered."

"I'm washing the dishes," I point out, not ready to go back out there.

Not yet and maybe not ever again.

"Do *not* hide." Her harshly spoken words make my back get tight. "Do not hide. You've done nothing wrong."

"I . . . I'm not hiding, Peggy," I lie. "I'm washing the dishes."

Getting even closer—so close I have no choice but to move away—she turns the water on, grabs the sponge from my hand, rinses it, then sets the pot to dry.

"Now you're done."

Looking at her and then at the pot, I shake my head. I turn the water back on to wash my hands. Figuring Peggy will stay until I obey, I follow her out to the front of the shop. The cute blonde is gone, but unfortunately, Antonio is not. When his anger-filled eyes find me, I fight the urge to bite my lip.

"I gotta head to the station in about an hour. Do you mind helping Hector close again tonight?" he asks.

"That's fine."

"Tomorrow I'm gonna talk to Dad about hiring someone else to help out so you don't gotta be here," he says.

Nausea turns my stomach while tears start to burn the back of my eyes.

"Are you saying that you're getting rid of me?"

I *can't* believe him. Seriously, I *cannot* believe him. Here, I'm happy. I feel fulfilled. And it's the kind of fulfillment that comes from hard work. I haven't had that feeling in a long time, and he wants to take it from me. If Peggy's right, he wants to take it from me because I have *a date*. A date that I don't even want to go on.

"You don't actually work here, Libby. You know that," he states.

My stomach twists, and my throat clogs.

"I like being here," I tell him, watching his jaw clench. "I know you don't get that because *you*"—I point at him—"obviously don't. But I"—I jerk my thumb at my chest—"I *like* being here. So, no. You're *not* going to talk to your dad about finding someone else. He doesn't need to worry about that right now, and neither does your mom. And if you don't like that, then too bad. You need to get over it, because I'm not going anywhere, Antonio."

"Libby—"

"Just stop," I hiss, leaning toward him. "God . . . just stop being a jerk."

I pull my eyes from his, feeling everyone else's eyes on me. I ignore them and go to the counter where we make pizzas. I check all the supplies. Noticing that some things are low, I start to refill them; then I make a list of things that need to be ordered, which is something that Martina normally does. Eventually, I go back out to the front of the shop and wipe down tables and chairs.

"He's gone, honey," Peggy says.

I look up from another table that I'm cleaning and find her, Marco, and Hector all watching me closely, looking worried.

"Libby . . . ," Marco calls. My eyes meet his. "We love having you here," he says.

Those stupid tears I have been fighting suddenly fill my eyes.

"*Chiquita,*" Hector says. I look at him, seeing him blurrily through my tears. "Marco's right. We love having you here."

"Thanks, guys," I say shakily while I wipe at my cheeks. I duck my head and get back to work, trying with all my might not to think about Antonio.

Chapter 4

Boiling Over

LIBBY

After knocking on Martina and Tony's front door, I peek through the side glass pane and smile when Martina's eyes meet mine. She called me at Christmas to tell me that she and Tony were home, so I made plans to see her before my blind date this evening.

"Cara!" She greets me with a smile when she opens the door, then reaches out and takes hold of me to pull me in for a hug. "How are you?"

"I'm good. How are you?" I ask, hugging her back just as tightly.

"We're home, so I'm happy," she answers as she leans back to smile at me. "Come on in. Tony's taking a nap, but we can have a cup of tea in the kitchen."

"Sounds good."

I follow her down a short hall, past a living room on the right and a half bath on the left. When we reach the kitchen at the end of the hall, she makes us each a cup of tea and then leads me into the dining room. Taking a seat at the dining room table, she sits close to me.

"Sugar? Milk?" she asks.

I take both from her, adding a dash of milk to my tea and a scoop of sugar.

"Thank you." I stir my tea, then sit back in my chair.

"How have things been going at the shop?"

"Busy like always, but between Antonio, Peggy, Hector, and Marco, things are going smoothly," I answer, hoping to reassure her.

"Antonio said you've been a big help," she says quietly.

Her words surprise me.

"I . . ."

"Has he been nice to you?"

No.

"Yes," I lie. "It's been good. There is nothing for you and Tony to worry about."

"We're selling the shop," she says suddenly, catching me off guard.

I cough on a gulp of tea I swallow down the wrong pipe.

"Wh-what?" I ask as she pats my back hard.

"The doctors don't want Tony going back to work, not for a while. They're still very worried about him."

"I thought he was okay," I whisper.

Her face softens as she reaches out and takes my hand.

"He's okay, *cara*, but owning a business is stressful. He cannot have that kind of stress in his life. Not now. Not ever again."

"I understand. What does Antonio think?"

"Tony wanted to hand over the shop to Antonio to run full-time." She pauses, pulling in a breath. "But our son has never been interested in running the pizzeria. He loves his job as a fireman. He'd never be happy running the shop. Plus, he's seen the toll the business has taken on his father."

I give her hand a squeeze, hating the turmoil I see in her eyes.

"And we're not getting any younger. We had plans—plans to travel and see the world, but we haven't done any of those things. Tony getting sick has made me realize what we have missed out on. I don't want us to miss out on anything more."

"So you're really going to sell?"

"Yes, we have an appointment to meet with a Realtor in a couple of days. We rent the space in the building, but we own everything in the shop. Hopefully it won't take long to find a buyer."

"How does Tony feel about this?"

"He's devastated, but he knows that if he keeps going like he's been going, he won't be around much longer. More than he wants the shop, he wants to watch Antonio find a woman and start a family of his own someday."

"I hate that there won't be a Tony's anymore. That I won't get to go into the shop to hang out with you," I tell her softly, and wet fills her eyes.

"Just because there won't be a Tony's doesn't mean our relationship will come to an end. I still expect you over for tea and gossip regularly."

I laugh. "You can count on that," I agree, taking another sip of tea as she does the same.

"Peggy says you have a date tonight."

Okay, Peggy has a big mouth.

"I do." I shift uncomfortably in the chair, not wanting to talk to her about it.

"She also mentioned that Antonio didn't seem very happy about you having that date."

"Martina . . . ," I sigh, and she smiles before taking a sip of her tea.

"I'm old, *cara*. Don't crush my dreams yet. Let me pretend that my son is finally seeing what I have seen for years."

Yes, Peggy has a very big mouth, and yes, she and Martina are both nuts for thinking that something is going to happen between Antonio and me.

"Don't get your hopes up."

"One thing I know, *cara*, is there is always hope," she says quietly.

I sigh again, then listen to her laugh.

Thankfully, after that she drops all talk about Antonio. I fill her in on the life and times of Fawn and Mackenzie because a lot has happened in the last month with both of my sisters, including Fawn getting engaged at Christmas and Mackenzie meeting Wesley, who's completely crazy for her.

~

Standing on the sidewalk outside the restaurant where I'm meeting my date, I catch my reflection in the window. I inhale deeply and then let out a long breath. I'm not nervous about dinner. I know from past experience not to have high hopes for how the night will go. I also learned a long time ago not to put too much effort into dressing up—every time I've gotten home from one of these dates, I've been annoyed with myself for spending so much time on my appearance.

I settle on a pair of tight black slacks and a simple, sheer black blouse. I tuck it into my pants so it's clear that my red belt matches my red heels. I keep my makeup simple, just adding untinted lip gloss to my lips. I wear my hair up in a bun, with a few wisps framing my face. Stepping into the restaurant, I scan the crowd. Palo said that my date, Walter, would meet me at the bar. He promised I couldn't miss him because he's movie-star handsome and really tall, with dirty-blond hair and striking blue eyes.

"Libby?"

A warm hand touches my arm, and I look up into a pair of blue—very blue—eyes.

Okay, so Palo was right.

The guy is handsome and very tall; even in my heels, he towers over me. He smells good, like subtle cologne and soap, and his gray-blue suit is killer and fits him like it was made for him. Judging by the quality, it probably was.

"Hi." I smile at him.

"Well, Palo didn't disappoint. You are as beautiful as he said you were."

Okay. Wow. He's handsome and sweet.

"Thank you." I duck my head, feeling my cheeks get warm.

He chuckles. "Our table should be ready." He places his hand against the small of my back and leads me toward the host. "Table for Yorks," he says.

The woman standing behind the podium looks down at the iPad in her hand, touches a few buttons on the screen, and smiles at both of us.

"Follow me." She picks up three menus, then leads us through the crowded restaurant.

The place is nice—maybe nicer than any restaurant I've been to before. The ambience is romantic, with beautiful artwork in nice frames hanging on the walls, each piece individually lit. The overhead lighting is dimmed to create intimacy, and the tables are all covered by white linen tablecloths.

"Here you are." The hostess stops at a small table in the back of the restaurant.

"Thank you," I say softly, and she smiles at me and then at Walter.

I slip off my coat and hang it on the hook near our table, then feel my lips part in astonishment when Walter gets close and holds my chair out for me. As I sit down, I watch him take his own seat across from me. I notice that he gave me the "good" view—where I can see the entire room. Soaking that in, I start to wonder if maybe this date might have actually been a good idea after all. As soon as I have that thought, though, Antonio pushes his way into my head. I grit my teeth and shove him right back out.

"The wine list." The hostess nods as she sets it on the table, then does the same with the dinner menus. "Your waiter will be with you shortly."

"Thank you," Walter and I say at the same time before we watch her disappear.

"Palo tells me you do makeup and hair," Walter says, picking up his napkin and resting it on his lap.

"I do." I pick up my napkin and do the same, trying to remember if I have ever eaten at a place with fancy napkins before.

"Do you like it?"

"I used to. Now I don't. Not really, anyway." I admit the truth before I can think better of it. "I . . ."

"Why's that?" He studies me, and I lean on the table with my elbows to answer, then quickly pull them back as I catch him smile.

I might not have ever eaten at a place as nice as this, but I'm pretty sure there is a rule somewhere about elbows on the table. And in a place like this, I'm sure elbows would be frowned upon.

"I'm not sure." I shrug. "I used to love it. Now I just don't feel that way. Don't get me wrong—I *enjoy* my job. I love working for Palo. I just don't know if it's what I want to do with the rest of my life."

"So what do you think you *do* want to do with the rest of your life?" he asks.

I sit back in my chair, realizing that twice in my life I've felt fulfilled and truly happy. And that both those times were when I was working at a pizza parlor.

"Maybe own a pizza parlor?" I admit.

His head tips to the side.

"Those are two vastly different things—making pizzas and doing makeup."

"I know," I agree, then I clear my throat. "So what do *you* do?"

"I'm a plastic surgeon." I can totally see that. He's perfect-looking, all beauty and class—from his hair to his custom suit to the expensive watch on his wrist and his polished shoes.

Why-oh-why can't I have a thing for fancy suits and polished shoes? Why do I have to be obsessed with worn T-shirts, faded jeans, and boots?

"Do you like it?" I ask, shoving Antonio out of my head once more.

"I do," he says. I can tell by the light that hits his eyes that there is more to it than him just being a plastic surgeon for socialites.

"Why?" I question.

His expression softens. "I specialize in reconstructive surgery for children. There is nothing better than changing the life of a child with a deformity, knowing that I've had a hand in making them feel better about themselves."

"That's amazing," I say quietly, knowing that's an understatement. In today's world, looks seem to be everything, and I'm sure that he's making a huge difference in the lives of the children he helps.

"Thank you."

"So tell me . . . how do you know Palo?"

"He's been doing my mom's hair for years. The last time I came into town, we got to talking, and he told me that there was a woman I needed to meet the next time I was in the city. Here we are."

"You don't live here?"

"I live in Los Angeles."

Of course he does. Of course the first blind date I've been on that doesn't have me wanting to sneak out the window in the bathroom is with a man who lives all the way across the country.

"Have you ever been?"

"No, I've lived my entire life in New York. I grew up on Long Island, and my dad's a cop. He worked a lot, so we didn't get to travel much when I was younger."

"You need to experience LA at least once in your life."

"Why's that?"

"The weather is nicer, the beaches are beautiful, and we have some of the best restaurants in the world."

"And movie stars?" I say, watching him laugh.

"There's also that," he agrees.

"Maybe someday I'll make my way over there."

His face softens right before the waiter comes over to ask us for our drink orders.

~

"Thank you for dinner," I tell Walter as we leave the restaurant. "I had a really nice time."

"Why do I feel like I'm not going to see you again?" he asks.

I bite the inside of my cheek.

"I . . ."

God, I've had such a great time with him. He's so easy to talk to, so easy to be around. But I know he's not what I want.

"I'm sorry." I duck my head. "I . . . There's a guy."

I feel his body tense, and I look up at him.

"He hates me." I laugh without humor as tears fill my eyes. "Well, I'm pretty sure he hates me, anyway, and I've had a crush on him forever. It's stupid because he's a jerk. Still . . ."

"Shit," he mutters.

I press my lips together. "I know it's stupid. Believe me, I know it is." I shake my head and look down at the sidewalk. "I just . . ."

"Follow your heart, Libby." His softly spoken words cut me off and pull my attention back to him. "It kills me to say that after sitting across from you and enjoying your company for the last two hours, but follow your heart." He touches his lips to my cheek. "If that guy doesn't see how amazing you are, fuck him. You can find better."

"Thank you, Walter." I smile up at him, and his eyes scan my face for a long moment before he shakes his head and takes my elbow gently in his hand.

He leads me to the edge of the sidewalk; then he raises his hand for a cab. When one pulls up, he helps me into the back seat and gives me another soft kiss on my cheek before he shuts my door. Waving at him through the window, I flash him an awkward smile before the cab pulls away from the curb.

Sitting forward, I wonder what's wrong with me. The date was awesome. No, better than awesome. Still, there were a hundred moments throughout dinner that I thought about Antonio. I couldn't even think about exploring things with Walter.

When the cab pulls up outside my building, I get out and head into my empty apartment. The space seems even quieter than it has since Mac started staying the night with Wesley. It makes me feel suddenly lonely. I think about taking a long hot bath but instead change into my pajamas, get a glass of wine, and plant myself in front of the TV. I watch a scary movie until I eventually fall asleep.

~

"So . . . ?" Peggy asks as soon as Hector and Antonio are out of earshot.

"So . . . what?" I play dumb and hand a customer the pizza he ordered.

Rolling her eyes, she shakes her head. "Your blind date! How did it go?"

"It was good." I shrug.

"Good?" she prods, tipping her head to the side and studying me.

"Walter was nice and sweet . . . and . . . well . . ." I pause, shrugging again. "The date went great, but he lives in LA and . . ."

"And Antonio?" she guesses.

I nod, and for some stupid reason, I feel like I'm going to cry.

"Oh, honey."

"I'm okay." I shake off the feeling, refusing to give in to it. I'm not even sure when I started to care so much about him.

"Right . . . ," she says, but I can tell that she doesn't actually believe me. "It will be okay."

"Yeah," I agree.

Not wanting to talk about it anymore, I grab a rag and busy myself with cleaning tables. After that, I help Hector make pizzas and set up orders until we close. Around ten, Antonio finally comes out of the office to lock up. I go into the back kitchen to start washing the dishes that have piled up in the sink throughout the evening.

"See you tomorrow." Peggy pokes her head through the door to the back kitchen, and I smile at her.

"See you tomorrow. Have a good night."

"You, too, honey."

"Later, *chiquita*!" Hector calls loudly.

"Later, Hector!" I shout back.

Peggy smiles once more, then disappears from the doorway.

"You can go, too," Antonio says, stepping into the kitchen where I'm still washing dishes.

"I'm almost done," I point out unnecessarily since he can see that I only have a few more things to wash.

"I can handle the rest."

"And so can I." I turn my back on him and get back to washing, doing it loudly on purpose and banging the dishes in the metal sink as I wash them.

"How was your date?"

"It was good. Walter was nice."

"Walter?" He spits out the name, and I turn to look at him.

"Yes. Walter," I repeat, locking my eyes with his and feeling my heart start to pound strangely against my rib cage. My knees go weak as the air around us changes. It seems to fill with electricity that causes the small hairs on the nape of my neck to stand on end.

"Did you sleep with him?"

"Is that *any* of your business?" I hiss, leaning toward him.

"Did you?" he growls.

Anger—along with something else I can't identify—fills the pit of my stomach.

"That's none of your business." I toss the sponge in my hand at him, and it lands against his chest with a wet thud before falling to the floor. His eyes go to where it landed, then slowly lift to meet mine. They darken.

Backing up, I look around for a way to escape.

Crap.

"There's nowhere to run," he says.

My eyes fly to his again. "Stay back." I grab the spray nozzle from the sink and raise it toward him with my fingers on the trigger.

"Put it down, Libby."

"No."

"Put it down," he demands.

I press the trigger, and water hits him in the chest. His eyes narrow; then he lunges at me.

I swear . . . I *swear* I don't know what happens next . . . One second we're both fighting to get control of the water, and the next, everything has boiled over.

We both move at the same time. His arms go around me tight, mine doing the same in return. His tongue thrusts into my mouth, and I follow his lead. Our mouths are nipping, licking, biting, fighting for supremacy. Our hands explore, mine up his shirt and his up mine. My back hits the wall next to the door, and his mouth leaves mine and begins traveling down my neck. Whimpering deep in my throat, I tip my head to the side to give him more access while my hands travel up the smooth, hard, warm skin of his back.

"Fuck. You smell good but taste better."

He nips my neck, and I score his back with my nails and listen to him groan in approval. His hands move to my ass, and he lifts, picking me up off the ground. Surrounding him with my legs, I drop my mouth back down to his while he carries me through the dimly lit shop to the office. Laying me on the couch, he comes down on top of me.

Things go from wild to frenzied. His hands move under my T-shirt; then it's gone. I do the same with his, tossing it to the floor. Leaning back, he traces the lace edge of my bra with his fingers and then tugs it down, dips his head, and pulls my nipple into his warm mouth, sucking hard. I cry out, raising my hips into his and grinding myself against him as he cups my neglected breast, pulling at my nipple through the lacy material. My core clenches, and my mind starts to catch up with what's happening as he kisses down my stomach to the edge of the jeans I have on.

"Antonio," I whisper.

He lifts his head, his dark, lust-filled eyes meeting mine. Unhooking the button to my jeans, he pulls down the zipper and then tugs my jeans and panties down my hips.

Oh god.

My mind goes blank. I forget everything and arch into him when his fingers touch me where no one ever has.

"Wet," he rumbles, sliding his fingers through my folds. My body locks as he starts to slide one finger inside of me.

"I'm a virgin," I whisper.

I watch in horror as his whole body gets tight. His eyes close down right before mine.

"What?" He pushes off the couch quickly. Standing, he looks down at me, his chest and abs heaving with each deep breath he takes.

"I . . . oh god." I cover my face with my hands, wishing I could disappear. "I'm sorry . . . I . . ."

"Jesus," he says softly. I pull my hands from my face and sit up, dragging my jeans back up over my hips. Tears start to fill my eyes when he turns his back on me and lifts his hands to his hair, tugging it. "Fuck me. What the fuck was I thinking?"

What was he thinking? Oh god.

Humiliated, I look around. I pick up the first shirt I see, then I toss it away like it's on fire when I see that it's his. I find mine and pull it down over my head. I stand and look around for my stuff. I put on my coat and grab my bag, then move as quickly as I can to the door. I don't look back. I don't stop to talk to him. I get out of there, running on my heels as fast as my legs will take me. When I get to the door, I fumble with the lock and whimper in distress when I can't get it open.

I feel Antonio get close, and I back up three steps when he reaches out for me.

"Libby."

"Don't." I keep my eyes from his, locking them on the floor near his feet. "Please don't. Please just open the door so I can go," I whisper as tears start to roll down my cheeks.

"Princess," he says softly, reaching out toward me again. I take another hasty step back.

"Don't." I look up at him, and he flinches. "Don't."

"I'll walk you home."

"I don't need you to walk me home."

"Honey, let me get my coat. Let me walk you home. We can talk."

"Open the door!" I scream, knowing I look insane but not caring at all. I'm so embarrassed, so humiliated. I need to get out of here now. "Please open the door so I can just go." I drop my eyes and see him move, then I hear the door open.

Careful not to touch him, I leave the restaurant. When I make it home, I stand in the foyer, breathing heavily, before rushing upstairs to my apartment. I pour a glass of wine to settle my nerves, then take it with me to the bathroom. I fill up the tub and get in, hoping to forget that tonight ever happened.

Chapter 5

CHALLENGE

ANTONIO

Leaning back in my dad's old office chair in front of his worn wooden desk, I look around at the pictures and newspaper clippings framed on the walls. I loved this place when I was a little kid, but once I started growing up, I began to resent it. I used to hate spending my days after school right here, in this chair, doing my homework. I hated that I couldn't go home after school like a normal kid or have dinner at home with my parents like all the other kids I knew did. As the years went on and my dad started to age, my resentment toward this place only got stronger. I could see the effect the pizzeria was having on my dad. He was too stubborn to hire more people to help him out. I guess I won't have to worry about that anymore since it's now going to be sold to someone else and will be someone else's problem to deal with.

Fuck . . .

As relieved as I am to know I won't have to watch this place slowly kill my dad, I *am* still going to miss it. It's a part of me. It's a part of almost every memory I have.

Rubbing my hand down my scruffy jaw, my eyes land on the couch against the wall. I flinch. Yeah, there are a lot of memories in this place—some better than others.

Libby . . .

Libby, the sexiest woman I have ever met in my life, is a virgin. When that information came out of her mouth, I swear to god my mind screamed, *Mine!* It freaked me the hell out. I've wanted her from the moment we met, but I thought I could never go there, not with her. I know women like her. I was in love with a woman just like her. One who needed the best of everything. One who wanted things I couldn't give her—including a life I didn't want for myself. When she ended things between us, she told me my dreams weren't her dreams, that she couldn't be happy with the life I could provide for us, that she wanted more. She had begged me to take over the shop from my dad when she overheard him and me talking about it. She wanted me to start a franchise, to build the family business so that I could give her a house in the city and an endless amount of money to buy whatever designer shit she thought she needed. I never wanted to run the shop. I wanted to be a firefighter. I wanted to help protect the city I love. I found out a few weeks after we broke up that she had been seeing some hotshot lawyer on the side, a man who had the kind of money to give her the life she wanted. Unfortunately for her, the guy was already married and wasn't at all interested in divorcing his wife for his sidepiece. In my opinion, she got what was coming to her.

Shaking my head, I scrub my hands down my face and then pull them away when the door to the office opens up.

Libby steps inside. Her wide, surprise-filled eyes lock with mine. My breath freezes in my lungs. I force myself to stay where I am when all I want to do is go after her, pin her to the couch, and finish what we started. I haven't seen her since the night everything between us went to shit. I had followed her home—without even putting on a jacket or locking up the shop—so I could make sure she made it home okay. She was so upset that she didn't even notice I was there.

"Hey," she says quietly.

I watch in awe as her cheeks turn an adorable shade of pink. Fuck, she's beautiful. So fucking pretty that she almost doesn't seem real. She has the kind of beauty you'd expect to see on the cover of a magazine or on TV, not working at a salon or a pizza parlor.

I lean forward in the chair, causing it to squeak. She jumps slightly at the noise.

"You haven't returned any of my calls."

Fuck! Why did I say that, even if it's the truth?

I've been frustrated for the last few days by not being able to get ahold of her when all I wanted to know is if she was okay.

"I don't think we have anything to talk about."

"You're wrong." I bite back a growl of frustration when she turns away from me, drops her bag onto the couch, and slips off her jacket. I walk around the edge of the desk and lean against it, crossing my arms over my chest in an attempt to try and get myself under control. "We should talk about what happened."

"We shouldn't." She spins around to face me. "I don't want to talk about that. Not now, not ever."

"We're going to talk about it, Libby," I say softly.

"No, we're not," she vows.

Then I notice her shoes.

"Where are your heels?" I lift my head to look at her.

"What?" Her perfectly shaped brows pull together over her beautiful eyes.

"Your heels. Why are you wearing sneakers?"

"Sheesh. Can't a girl wear sneakers without everyone questioning her?" she asks.

I wonder jealously who else might have pointed out that she's wearing sneakers instead of the heels that are always on her feet.

"I need to get out front. Peggy needs help."

She starts for the door, but I step in front of her and block her path. I watch her face pale and her chest start to rise and fall rapidly. Dropping my eyes to her mouth, I take a step toward her. She takes a step back, putting her hand up as heat crackles between us.

"Antonio . . ."

"Yeah?"

"What are you doing?" she whispers.

My eyes focus on her worry-filled ones.

"I'm wondering what will happen if I kiss you again."

"You're *not* kissing me again," she says firmly, with a shake of her head. She takes another step back.

"I might." I take another step toward her. "Unless you're going to use that mouth of yours to talk to me."

"We're not talking, either."

"Then I'm going to kiss you."

"No, you are not." She looks around the office, trying to find a way to get away from me.

"Then talk to me," I growl.

Her jaw clenches.

"What do you want to talk about?" she finally asks, seeing there is no way out.

"You know what I want to talk about."

"Yeah, I know. But instead, I think we should talk about the way you've been such a jerk to me. The way you've made me feel like crap because . . . because of the way I dress, because I wear makeup and heels. Or maybe you want to talk about the way you treated me after . . ." Her cheeks get darker. "After I told you what I told you. How about we talk about all of *that*?" she suggests.

My chest gets tight.

Yeah, I fucked up royally with her. No doubt about it.

"Libby . . ." I reach for her, but she steps to the side before I can touch her.

"Like I said, I don't think we have anything to talk about."

"We do. You caught me off guard, and—"

"Stop." She shakes her head, cutting me off. "I don't want to do this tonight. Please," she whispers.

Seeing the tiredness and defeat in her eyes, my gut tightens right along with my chest.

"I'll give you time," I agree. "But we're going to talk, Libby."

"Fine." She nods. "Now will you move out of my way so I can get to work? It's New Year's Eve, and there is already a line of people out the door."

Stepping aside, I let her go even though every instinct is telling me not to. When the door closes behind her, I run my fingers through my hair.

Fuck. I want her.

I've wanted her for a long fucking time, but I've done jack shit about it besides push her away. Now I need to see if I can somehow undo that damage. At that thought, I smile. I have always loved a good challenge—and I know that Libby is going to be just that.

I open the door to the office, then lock it behind me and go to the back of the shop, where Libby is making pizzas with Hector.

Meeting Hector's gaze, I nod toward him. "I got this if you want to help Marco."

I watch his eyes go to Libby. He looks at her with a question in his eyes.

"It's okay," she tells him.

My jaw clenches as he lifts his chin and then moves to the opposite side of Libby. Like it's happened every time I've worked with her, we fall right into sync.

Her sister Mackenzie told me that Libby was a hard worker, but I didn't believe her. All I saw were Libby's expensive clothes and her perfectly styled hair and makeup. I thought she was just like my ex, that all she cared about was money. I was wrong about her. There is no way in hell my ex would ever have stepped in to help out like Libby has. If she had been forced to help, she would have complained the entire time. I've *never* heard Libby complain—not even once. She's never complained about washing dishes, busing tables, or making pies. She doesn't say that she's tired, but I know she must be from working two jobs most days. Instead, she's always smiling, always happy. As if she wouldn't rather be anywhere else than right here, working and getting her hands dirty. Looking at her profile and the frown I put on her face, I fight the urge to sigh. Yeah, I was wrong about her. Now I need to prove to her that I'm not the jerk I've shown myself to be more than once. I have my work cut out for me. If someone ever treated me the way I've treated her, they would see my back—and nothing else ever again. I just hope she's not as bitter and fucked-up as I am.

The first time I saw her at the shop, she was with her sisters. They were sitting at one of the booths in the back. I couldn't take my eyes off her. I noticed that she had been having the same problem with looking at me. I had been about to make my approach and introduce myself to her when I overheard her talking to her sisters about some designer bag she wanted. Hearing that was like a bucket of cold water hitting me in the face. After that, I shoved her right in the same box as my ex. Looking at her once more now, I just hope that I can find a way to convince her to forgive me.

I see a smile light up her face, and I'm surprised when she suddenly stops what she's doing and slides a half-made pizza to Hector to finish.

"Be right back," she tells him as she spins around. "Lucas! Madeline!" she shouts happily as she hurries past the counter. A little girl of probably four or five throws herself into Libby's arms and giggles while a man who's my age or maybe a few years older stands back, watching them embrace with a smile on his face. The moment the little girl lets go, Libby's eyes go to the guy. Her expression fills with a sweetness I haven't seen before. She wraps her arms around his waist. Jealousy, hot and ugly, turns my stomach and warms my blood as I watch them.

"You okay, *amigo*?" Hector questions.

I pull my gaze off Libby to look at him.

"I'm good."

"You sure?" He drops his eyes to my hands, and I realize the ball of dough I have in my grasp has been mangled by my clenched fists.

I shake my hands and narrow my eyes at Hector and Marco, who are both smirking at me.

"What?" Neither of them says anything, and both of them get back to work. Pressing out another crust, I look over my shoulder at Libby. She's coming back behind the counter, and the man and girl are walking out the door with a pizza that they must have called in for pickup.

"Who was that?" I ask when our eyes meet and her step falters.

"That's Fawn's fiancé's brother and his daughter."

Her words catch me off guard, and I stare at her for a long moment. I've known both of her sisters for years, but until recently I didn't even know that either of them was dating anyone serious.

"Fawn's *engaged*?" I ask.

Her startled eyes dart from the pizza she's dusting with cheese to meet mine.

"She got engaged at Christmas."

"What?" I ask, watching her smile.

"Levi, Fawn's boyfriend, asked her to marry him Christmas morning," she says, dropping her eyes back to the pizza in front of her.

"Didn't they just start dating?" I ask, remembering Libby and some guy coming in for pizza not long after Halloween.

"Yeah."

"Don't you think that's a little quick to suddenly be engaged?"

"They're in love. What does it matter if they get engaged now or a year from now? I think when you want to spend the rest of your life with someone, you should spend the rest of your life with them—especially when you don't know how long your life will be."

"That sounds like a line out of a romance movie," I say, remembering her aversion to romantic movies and how adamant she was about disliking them.

She peeks up at me and shrugs one shoulder. "I guess it does."

"So you *do* like romance?" I nudge my shoulder against hers, and she rubs her lips together.

"I might not like romance movies, but I'm still a girl. I like the color pink, heels, makeup, and designer clothes. I also like the idea of falling in love and finding my own Prince Charming to build a life with one day. Who *doesn't* want to fall in love and live happily ever after?"

"I've been in love before. It's not all it's cracked up to be."

She licks her bottom lip. "Maybe you weren't in love with the right person."

I stare into her eyes, then clear my throat. "Yeah, maybe." I pull my eyes away from hers.

Really, there is no *maybe* about it. I shouldn't have fallen in love with my ex. I only saw what I wanted to see. I stupidly thought that, in time, she would change her ways. That if I could just love her enough she would see that material things weren't important, that family was all that mattered. I really believed she would eventually be happy with the life I was trying to build for us. In the end, I was just never enough.

~

"Two minutes until midnight!" Peggy shouts as I lock the door behind the last customer of the night and head toward the kitchen.

Marco pops a bottle of champagne. Lola takes it from him and starts to fill plastic champagne glasses. Seeing my parents standing there with their arms around each other, I smile. My dad looks good—better than he has in weeks. The worry lines around my mom's eyes have started to fade away. They both look happy, which is a relief. Dad's heart attack scared them both. I had never seen my mom cry so much or seen my dad look weak. He's always been strong. Having been together since they were eighteen, neither of them would know how to function without the other.

"Can I have some, Mom?" Peggy and Hector's daughter, Valeria, asks her as she eyes the bottle of champagne Lola is holding.

"When have I ever let you drink alcohol?" Peggy asks with a frown.

"Dad's let me have a sip of his beer before."

"Has he?" Peggy looks at Hector and raises a brow.

"It was only one time," he mutters, wrapping his bulky arm around Valeria's shoulder. "There's sparkling cider for you."

"Fine," she grumbles, taking a glass from her dad.

I smile at them, then head though the opening into the back kitchen. I grab a full champagne glass off the counter as the countdown on the TV plays loudly in the background. Moving next to Libby, I watch her eyes light up as she counts down along with the TV and everyone in the room.

"Nine. Eight. Seven. Six. Five. Four. Three. Two. One . . . Happy New Year!" everyone shouts, clinking their glasses together before taking sips and kissing.

Looking down at Libby, I feel her eyes on me. My stomach knots when our eyes lock.

"Happy New Year," she whispers.

I lean down and touch my lips to the corner of her mouth. She gasps before I pull away, murmuring, "Happy New Year, Princess."

Without another word to her, I go over to my parents and give them each a hug.

"I'm going to miss this place," Mom says quietly, looking around the space and at the people who have made Tony's what it is.

"I know you will. And I know Dad will, too, but it's time for you both to move on. It's time for you guys to relax and enjoy life. It's time for you two to do all that traveling you've been talking about," I say as my dad wraps his arm around my shoulder.

"You're right."

Dad smiles, and sadness fills my chest. I might not like this place or want to spend the rest of my life running a pizzeria, but I'm proud of my parents for what they have accomplished and for the life that they were able to provide for me by working here.

Chapter 6

PRINCESS

LIBBY

"What?" I sit up in bed with my cell to my ear, blinking against the bright light of my lamp when I flip it on.

"I got married!" Fawn repeats, sounding excited.

"I thought you were in Vegas," I say, trying to wake up enough to understand exactly what she's trying to tell me.

"We *are* in Vegas." She laughs. "We also got married."

"Oh my god," I whisper.

"I know," she whispers back.

I can actually hear the happiness in her voice.

"I wish you and Mac could have been here."

"Me, too," I agree, still in shock. "Please tell me you have pictures."

"Tons of them. We even got a few of them with Elvis."

"Did Elvis *marry* you?" I ask while I wonder how she might have been able to talk badass Levi into that.

"No. Levi wouldn't go for it, so we had a regular wedding at a normal chapel. But I stopped an Elvis impersonator on the Strip and made him take a picture with us."

She laughs, and a smile twitches my lips. I can just see her talking Levi into doing that.

"God, now *you're* married and *Mac's* pregnant," I say without think-ing. My eyes widen as I cover my mouth, hoping I can somehow shove the words back inside.

"What?" she yells at the top of her lungs.

I slap my palm against my forehead.

"I . . . Crap. I shouldn't be the one to tell you this, because it's Mac's news. She found out yesterday that she and Wesley are pregnant."

"Holy cow."

She can say *that* again. When I got home to do her hair and makeup for the New Year's Eve ball she and Wesley were attending, I found her locked in the bathroom with five positive pregnancy tests on the coun-ter. She was sitting on the floor in shock.

"Mom's going to be over the moon. A son-in-law *and* a grandbaby— all in a year," I mutter, picking at a thread on my comforter. Secretly, I'm a little depressed that my sisters are moving on with their lives while I'm stuck doing nothing with mine.

"Holy cow," she repeats.

I sigh. I really should have kept my mouth shut.

"Is Mac okay?"

I close my eyes, remembering Mac resting her hand against her stomach and already looking in love.

"Yeah. She's freaked, but happy about the news. She's worried about telling Wesley," I admit softly.

"Why is she worried? He'll be happy about the baby."

"I know, but it's still early in their relationship."

"True. But then again, everything happens when it should," she says quietly.

I inhale sharply. "You're right," I agree.

"I should let you get back to sleep. I'm sure you need to get up early for work."

"Yeah. I love you. Give Levi a hug from me, and tell him I said congrats."

"I will. When we get home, we're going to have a big party to celebrate."

"Sounds good. Don't have too much fun in Vegas," I say.

Levi says something to her in the background that makes her start to giggle. I smile into the phone, then laugh as it goes dead in my hand.

I shut off my lamp and lie back down, holding my cell phone. I wonder when the heck my sisters and I grew up. It doesn't seem like it was that long ago that we were all living in this apartment, a bunk bed and a twin bed shoved in this tiny bedroom, each of us fighting over the bathroom in the mornings to get ready for work or school. We never really stopped to think about what the future would hold. I bet neither Mac nor Fawn would have guessed that in a few short years they would be settling down and starting families of their own. I know *I* wouldn't have guessed that I would be sitting here contemplating my life and what I should be doing with the rest of it. I used to think that because I loved all things beauty, I would be happy doing makeup and hair. Now I know I won't be. I know that eventually I'm going to end up hating my job, no matter how much money I make. I don't want that. I don't want to spend the rest of my life being miserable just so I can live comfortably.

Then again, everything happens when it should.

Fawn's words echo in my mind.

"It's a new year, Libby. Maybe it's time to risk it all and go for broke," I say into the dark.

My stomach twists with excitement and nerves.

Yes, I think as I close my eyes and a smile curves my lips. *It's time to take a chance on something new.*

∼

"*Cara!* What a nice surprise." Martina gives me a warm smile after opening the door.

"I know I should have called before I showed up, but I need to talk to you and Tony. Is he around?"

"Is everything okay?" She studies me, the smile she was wearing moments ago sliding off her face. Concern fills her eyes.

"Yeah, everything's great." I smile, hoping to reassure her. "I just want to discuss something with you both if you have time."

"Okay, come on in. Tony's in the dining room." She lets me into the house and closes the door before she leads me to Tony, who is sitting with a cup of tea in front of him—along with an open newspaper.

"Hey, Tony," I say when he notices me. He smiles, then gets up to kiss my cheek and give me a hug.

"What brings you here?" he asks while I take a seat across from him and Martina.

Feeling suddenly nervous, I blurt out my reason. "I want to buy Tony's."

Tony looks at me, stunned, while Martina's mouth drops open.

Last night, I couldn't stop thinking about what I want, what will make me happy. When I got up this morning, I called the Realtor who has the listing for Tony's and found out how much they were selling the business for. Then I made a few more calls and found out that I have just enough money saved for a down payment on the business and the rent for the space—but I would still need a backer. My dad has always been my biggest champion, so I called him with my idea and asked if he could help me out. He told me that he would help out in whatever way I needed. After I got off the phone with him, I got in a cab and came straight over.

"You *what?*" Tony asks, trying to make sure he heard me correctly.

I look around their cozy yellow dining room, getting my thoughts in order before I blurt out anything more.

"I want to purchase Tony's from you and Martina."

"*Cara*, you work as a stylist," Martina points out, looking worried about me.

"I do, but I don't really like it. I *love* working at Tony's. I'm happy there. I feel good about myself every time I step through the door. I feel proud and excited. I know it might seem strange because of the career I have built for myself as a makeup artist, but I love your shop. I love making pies. I want to keep working there. I want to keep feeling good and happy, and I'm happy there." I know I'm rambling and that I don't sound very sophisticated, as I probably should sound at a time like this.

"Owning a business is a lot of responsibility," Tony points out gently.

"I know it is. As Martina can tell you, I already have a business of my own. I started it from just an idea. I know this is not going to be easy, and I would not even be thinking about taking the risk if I didn't know I could handle it." When I finish, Tony's eyes go to Martina before coming back to me.

"Are you sure about this, *cara*?" Martina asks.

"Yes, I'm sure. I have never been more sure about anything in my life."

Even when I decided to move to the city to go to cosmetology school, I had doubts about what I was doing. But I have no doubts about this.

"Okay," Tony states. "We will all have to talk to our Realtor, and you will have to speak with the landlord of the building and figure out all the financing stuff. If you really want it, it's yours."

"Really?" I ask in disbelief.

"Really," he agrees.

Tears start to fill my eyes.

"I should tell Antonio," Martina says, studying me.

Unexpected panic fills my chest.

"No!" I shout, causing her to jump in her chair. "I mean"—I lower my voice—"not yet. Not until after everything is settled. Please. I don't want to jinx it."

The truth is that I don't want Antonio to try and talk me out of buying the shop because of his own personal feeling about the business.

"He knows we're selling, *cara*. It might make him happy to know that you're going to be the one purchasing it," Martina says.

I inhale.

"Please, not yet. Can we wait until everything is done?" I ask.

She looks at her husband, who is studying me with a strange look in his eyes.

"When the time's right, *you* can tell him," Tony says, putting emphasis on the word *you*.

That panic in my chest comes back, in full force.

"Okay, I'll tell him," I agree, *maybe* not lying.

I tell myself that I can just send him an email or a text to let him know, once everything is done.

"I like the idea of Tony's staying in the family," Martina says.

I smile at her warmly, liking the idea of her thinking of me as family. My eyes widen as she continues.

"Who knows? Maybe one day you will even have the last name Moretti."

"Martina . . . ," Tony sighs, "leave the poor girl alone."

"They say the person you ring in the New Year with will be the one you spend your year with."

I think back to Antonio telling me that we needed to talk, then kissing the side of my mouth.

"You're freaking her out." Tony rolls his eyes at his wife, and I shift uncomfortably.

Martina isn't freaking me out—I'm used to her seeing something that isn't there between Antonio and me. I do wonder exactly what it is that he wants from me, though, and what he thinks it is that we need to talk about.

Now *that* is totally freaking me out.

"I'm not freaking her out," Martina denies.

"Is she freaking you out?" Tony asks.

I shake my head. His eyes move to my hair, and I realize a little too late that I'm twisting a strand of hair around my finger.

Crap.

I've always done that when I'm lying. When I was younger, I thought my parents had magical powers because they always knew when I fibbed. I had no idea it was really because I would twirl my hair whenever I wasn't telling the truth.

"She'll be fine." Martina grins at me. "Anyway, do you have time to stay for breakfast? I was just going to make us some egg whites and toast."

I must make a face, because Tony starts to laugh. "Believe me—they *are* that bad."

"I'm sure they aren't. I bet Martina makes some awesome egg whites, but I need to get to the salon. I work today."

"I wish I had an excuse. I miss real eggs and coffee," Tony says.

Martina glares at him.

"What? I didn't say I was going to go out and eat them. But I *do* miss them."

"Too bad," she grumbles.

Giving her a hug, I say, "Again, I'm really sorry for just showing up without calling. I was so excited to ask you this when I woke up this morning."

"You're always welcome in our home, *cara*."

"Thanks." I let her go, then give Tony a quick hug before heading for the front door.

Once I'm outside, I catch a cab across town to work—with a big smile on my face.

∾

Time's up.

Staring down at the text message I just got from Antonio, I feel my pulse start to race.

What the hell does that mean?

I know I'm going to have to talk to him eventually, but I don't think I'm ready. Not yet.

What was I thinking?

His words from that night we almost had sex still hurt me every time they float through my mind.

"God. What the hell was *I* thinking?" I whisper to myself.

"What were you thinking about what?" Palo asks, making me jump.

I spin around in the makeup chair to face him.

"Nothing." I drop my cell phone into my purse.

"Love, you are the worst liar in the world." He slaps my hand, which I realize is toying with a piece of my hair.

Dammit.

"So tell me. What's going on?"

"I . . ."

I start to tell him that it's nothing. Then I realize that maybe, as a man, he can give me some insight into what's going on in Antonio's head.

"Well . . . do you remember Antonio?"

He nods, crossing his arms over his chest.

"You know I've had a crush on him forever."

Nodding again, Palo's eyes narrow slightly. He doesn't like Antonio because I've shared stories with him about how Antonio has acted toward me in the past. Since Palo is my friend—and a good one—he thought it was ridiculous that I still had a crush on him. He's made that perfectly clear by trying to set me up with every available man in the city.

"Well . . . we kinda kissed."

"You *kind of* kissed?" His eyes narrow farther.

"Well . . . we did more than kind of kiss," I admit reluctantly.

He suddenly pulls me from the chair by my hand.

"What are you doing?"

"We're going to talk—in the office."

He drags me through the salon to the office, where he shuts the door behind us. Leading me to one of the chairs, he forces me to sit and then takes a seat across from me. He leans in with his elbows on his knees. "Tell me *exactly* what happened."

"We kissed."

"You said that." He waves his hand around, indicating that he wants me to get to the point.

I bite my lip. "Fine . . . we kissed. I don't even know who started it. One minute we were arguing; then the next we were making out hot and heavy. He was picking me up and carrying me to the office in the pizza parlor. He laid me on the couch and took off my top," I say quickly. His eyes widen. "Umm"—I inhale, then look away from him before whispering—"I told him I was a virgin and he stopped. He shut down completely and said, 'What was I thinking?' I was so embarrassed by how he responded that I kind of lost my mind and freaked out."

"Jesus," he mutters.

I lift my head.

"When was this?"

"A few days before New Year's."

"Have you spoken to him since then?"

"Yes." I nod, feeling my cheeks get warm as I think about him saying he was going to kiss me again in the office and then him kissing me on New Year's Eve in front of everyone. Not that anyone noticed. "But I haven't talked to him about what happened. I told him I needed time. Today he sent me a text that just said, 'Time's up.'"

"Time's up?" he repeats.

I nod and shake my head. "I don't know what that means—exactly."

"My guess is your time's up."

I blink at him. "Okay, so what does that mean?"

"Hopefully it means he's got his head on straight. If it doesn't, it means that I'm going to pay him a visit."

"Palo . . . ," I sigh.

He shakes his head and reaches out to take my hands between both of his.

"I love you. I've listened to you talk about this guy since the day you started working for me. I know that you've had a crush on him, and I know he's been a dick to you—which is stupid since you are one of the sweetest women I know."

"Palo," I whisper, feeling my chest get warm at his words.

"I swear if I didn't like men I would make you mine. My mom would be thrilled beyond belief if I brought a girl like you home, but that's never going to happen. Still, this guy is an idiot for not taking anything you are willing to give him," he says.

My chest gets warmer.

"He's had his heart broken," I tell him, not even sure why that matters exactly. It's the only defense I have.

"Did *you* break his heart?"

"Well . . . no."

"Then he's just an idiot. You're not the one who hurt him. You're Libby! Sweet, beautiful Libby. He's a dick for treating you like crap."

"I love you," I blurt. His hands tighten around mine.

"Ditto, love, which is why I'm worried about you."

"I'll be okay," I assure him, not sure if I'm lying or not.

"I know, in the end, you will be. But I'm worried about the time between then and now. You like this guy. You have for a long time."

"I know . . . I also know I probably *shouldn't* like him," I admit.

"No, you shouldn't," he agrees.

This makes my stomach drop. He tugs my hands, forcing me closer.

"As much as it kills me to say it, you need to explore this. I'm worried about what will happen, but I know that if you *don't* explore this thing between you two, you will regret it and you won't be able to move on. So if he comes to you, listen to what he has to say, and *then* decide from there what to do."

Biting my lip, I think about what he's just said. I know he's right. I won't be able to move on until I figure out what's going on between Antonio and me. I'm also scared to hear what he has to say.

"I'll hear him out."

"Good." He gives my hands a squeeze. "Now I need to get back to work before Josie's hair falls out. I left her in foils in my chair."

I gasp. He *never* leaves a client.

"She'll be okay." He waves off my worried look and stands. "Are you done for the day?"

"I'm done here. I still need to run a few dresses back to clients," I say as I stand.

He nods in understanding.

"Get home safe. If you talk to Antonio tonight, I expect you to tell me everything he says when I see you tomorrow."

"I'll call," I say as he leans down to kiss my cheek before he leaves the office.

After leaving the salon, I head to one of my clients who lives just down the block. I drop off two dresses that she had rented out for New Year's. Then I head to the East Side and drop off three more dresses to another client. By the time my cab pulls up outside my place, it's already after eight in the evening. I'm not just tired—I'm exhausted. I haven't been sleeping well these last few days. Not with everything that has happened.

I unlock the door and go inside the apartment, stopping dead when I see Mackenzie lying on the couch in a pair of sweats and a baggy T-shirt.

"Hey." She lifts her head off the arm of the couch. I notice that her eyes are red and puffy. Then I see the mass of tissues that has collected on top of the coffee table.

"What's going on?"

I shut the door.

She starts to sob, covering her face with her hands.

"Is the baby okay?" I ask as my stomach fills with worry.

"The baby is fine," she whimpers, pulling her hands from her face.

"Is it Wesley?" I ask.

She covers her face once again and cries harder, making me worry about Wesley's reaction to her being pregnant. I hope he didn't say something about not wanting the baby. I resolve that if he did, I'll get in a cab to go kick his ass.

Shrugging off my coat, I take a seat on the couch next to her and pull her into my arms.

"What happened?"

I rub her back and listen to her tell me about the fight she and Wesley got into this morning. A fight based on him saying that he wants to marry her but refusing to open up to her about his past. After she finishes telling me, I hold on to her as she cries. I try to comfort her. Eventually I help her up and get her into bed. Then I lie with her, listening to her tears as she continues to cry. In my gut, I know that she and Wesley will be okay—they love each other. Eventually they will find a way to work through this. Wesley will find a way to make this right. He looks at my sister like she's the reason he's breathing, so he will do whatever he needs to do. I just hate that they have to go through this right now—especially after just finding out they're pregnant. Once Mac is finally asleep, I carefully get out of her bed and go to the bathroom. I change into pajamas, wash my face, and brush my hair. I leave the bedroom and shut the door, then get my cell phone so I can order some food. Seeing a text message from Antonio, I click on it as my pulse speeds up.

You haven't texted me back. Is everything okay?

Sorry, everything is fine. I was just busy with work.

That's okay. I'm on call this week at the station, but I was wondering if you will have dinner with me next Friday night? Seven?

I stare at the message, not sure how to reply. Part of me wants to jump at the chance to have dinner with him. The other part of me is freaked out at the prospect of having dinner with him. I don't want him to do or say something that will hurt me again.

Risk it all . . . I remind myself quietly as I type my reply.

Sure, where do you want to meet?

I'll pick you up at your place. We'll go from there to the restaurant.

I'd rather meet you at the restaurant.

And I'd rather pick you up.

You're annoying . . . Fine, I'll see you at seven.

I press "Send," then watch a little bubble appear, letting me know he's writing me back again.

See you then, Princess. Sweet dreams.

Don't call me Princess.

I type this quickly and press "Send" before calling in an order for shrimp fried rice. I have another message from him when I hang up my call. My heart thumps even harder as I read it.

You're a girl who likes the color pink, heels, makeup, and designer clothes. A girl who wants to fall in love with your very own Prince Charming. You're the definition of a princess.

Oh my god. He remembered what I said . . . almost word for word.
I have no comeback, so I type a vague response quickly.

Good night, Antonio. Be safe at work.

Thanks, baby.

Baby . . . ?
I stare at that one word while my stomach twists with anxiety. I know I can handle jerky Antonio—I've been dealing with him for years. I just don't know if I have the strength to handle him being sweet, then letting me down by being a jerk once more. Biting my lip, I go to the fridge and pour myself a glass of wine. After I take a seat on the couch, I turn on the TV and flip through channels for something to watch while I wait for my food to arrive. I somehow end up being captivated by some stupid romantic comedy. As I watch, I root for the guy to figure out that he's in love with the girl early on so she can get her happily ever after without the drama. Not surprisingly, it doesn't happen. Still, in the end, it all works out.

Chapter 7

I'll Keep Him Busy . . . Oh Lord

Libby

Hearing a knock on my apartment door, I look at the clock on my bathroom wall and see that it's 6:20. Antonio's early—as in *really* early. *Oh lord.*

My heart starts to race, and my palms start to sweat. Knowing it's now way too late to back out of dinner, I grab my robe and tie it tightly around my waist.

The last week has flown by in a flash with everything that has gone on. I've dealt with clients from Designer Closet, worked at the salon, met with the Realtor and the owner of the building the pizza parlor is in, spoken with a lawyer, and had discussions with the bank. I've also taken Mac to her prenatal appointment and played the go-between for her and Wesley. Thankfully, they're back together. I've also worked at Tony's a few times, and I had dinner with Palo last night to tell him that in two months, when I officially close on the pizzeria, I will no longer be working at the salon.

Palo was upset about my leaving, but happy for me all the same. I also had tea with Miss Ina this morning, who was funny and sweet in her grumpy-old-woman way.

"Coming!" I shout, jolting myself out of my thoughts. I don't even bother looking through the peephole; I just unlatch the lock and open it. I start to tell Antonio that I'm not dressed, that he will have to wait for me. My mouth drops open when I see my mother standing outside my door.

"Mom?" I frown.

What's she doing here?

She lives on Long Island, so it's not like she just drops by often.

"Libby." She moves past me, tosses her purse on the couch, then takes off her coat and tosses it, too, before she crosses her arms over her snowflake-embroidered, sweater-covered chest.

"What's going on? What are you doing here? Is everything okay? Where's Dad?" I ask, each question in rapid succession. I don't even stop to take a breath.

"Apparently there's a *lot* going on. I'm here because my youngest daughter is keeping secrets from me. Everything is *not* okay, but your father is at home, in front of the TV where I left him."

"Is this about the pizzeria?" I ask, figuring that's the only thing I've kept from her.

Okay . . . so I haven't told her about Antonio, but technically there is nothing to tell.

"Yes, it's about the pizzeria!" she shouts, uncrossing her arms and planting her hands on her hips.

"Mom . . ."

"Do not 'Mom' me, Libby Alice Reed. You went to your dad and asked him to help you, and you didn't even mention anything about it to *me*."

"I was going to tell you," I say, shifting uncomfortably.

"When? I've known about it for a week now, and you still haven't even mentioned it, although we've talked every *day!*" She shouts the last word.

"I'm sorry. I've been a little busy." I hold my hands out in front of me in a placating manner, hoping to calm her down. Her eyes move to my hands, then drop down the length of me and narrow.

"Busy doing what? And why are you getting dressed up? Where are you going?"

Oh lord.

I do not want to tell my mom that I have a date tonight. Seeing as how she's standing in my living room and Antonio is supposed to be here soon, though, I realize I probably won't have a choice.

"Ugh . . ."

"That is not an answer."

"I have a date."

I bite the inside of my cheek.

"A *date?*"

"Yes, a date. And he's supposed to be here soon, so if you could please get out whatever it is you need to say about the pizzeria before he comes, that would be awesome. He doesn't know that I'm going to buy it—and I don't want him to know about it yet."

"Why don't you want him to know?"

Crap.

"I . . . well . . . it's his parents' shop. And . . ." I pause, trying to get my thoughts in order. "Everything has been a little weird between us. I don't want to tell him I'm buying the shop and rock the boat. I know how he feels about the pizzeria, and I don't want him to try to talk me out of it."

"Seems to me you've gotten good at keeping secrets from people."

Have I?

I'm not sure. I know that lately I've been more closed off with things going on in my life, but I don't think I'm keeping secrets.

"Mom, I'm sorry I didn't tell you about the pizzeria. I promise I was going to tell you."

"You have always been open with me about everything," she says.

Guilt fills the pit of my stomach. I *have* always talked to her about anything and everything going on in my life. She never made me feel like I couldn't share—no matter what was going on or how embarrassed it might make me.

"You're right," I whisper.

"And . . ." She stops speaking when tears fill her eyes. "I feel like I'm losing each of you."

"You're not losing us, Mom."

I close the space between us and wrap my arms around her.

"Fawn got married in Vegas. *Vegas*, of all places! And then Mac finds out she's pregnant and doesn't tell me. While you . . . you buy a pizzeria and don't even mention it to me."

"I haven't bought it yet, Mom. It's a long process. There is a lot of paperwork before it'll be officially mine."

"Whatever. You know what I mean," she grumbles, sniffling.

"I think we are all just trying to figure out who we are on our own. Don't get me wrong—we love you. But sometimes you can be a bit overbearing when it comes to our lives and your opinions about them."

"Overbearing?" she whispers, sounding offended. I cringe, knowing that wasn't the right word to use with her, even if it *is* the correct word.

"You love us. It's normal for a mom who cares about her kids to be overbearing," I say, trying to soothe her.

She sighs.

"I do love you girls. I just want you to be happy."

"We're working on that, Mom. Each of us is just trying to figure out our own version of happiness."

"And making *pizzas* is going to make you happy? I thought you loved doing makeup and hair."

"Makeup and hair is something I'm good at, but I don't feel fulfilled doing it. Not anymore. It's not a challenge to me. I love working at Tony's. Each time I walk through the doors there, I get excited."

"It's just pizza . . . ," she says, sounding confused.

"I know, but it's also the idea of starting something on my own, doing things my way, and building a business that I'm proud of—one that I'll be proud to have my name attached to."

"You have always been determined to make a name for yourself in this world."

"I get it from you. *You* taught me to be independent, to go after what I want. To be confident about who I am."

"I did teach you that, didn't I?" she mutters, sounding pleased with herself.

I laugh. "Yes, you did."

"So you're really going to own a pizzeria in New York?"

"Hopefully . . . ," I say quietly.

Her expression shifts, and warmth fills her eyes. She rests her hand against my cheek. "I've always been proud of you. So has your dad."

"I know you both have."

"I love you, honey."

"I love you, too, Mom," I whisper back over the lump that has formed in my throat.

She wraps her arms around me again, and her hand smooths its way down my back. Eventually, she leans away to look at my face.

"Now tell me about the guy you're going out with tonight."

Laughing, I shake my head. "He's just a guy."

"Just a guy?" She narrows her eyes, and I sigh.

"He's a guy that I have had a stupid crush on forever."

"Antonio?" she says, sounding excited and surprised.

I realize then just how much I used to share with my mom. Maybe she's right—maybe I *have* gotten really good at keeping things to myself.

"Yes."

"Oh my," she whispers. Her eyes go to the clock on the wall in the kitchen. "What time is he coming?"

"Seven," I say, realizing that I now only have a few minutes to finish getting ready before he is supposed to arrive.

"You're not dressed."

"I know. I was getting dressed when you showed up." I wave my hand down my body at my robe.

"Go. Go get dressed. If he shows up, I'll keep him busy while he waits."

Oh lord.

"Mom . . ."

"It will be fine. Promise." She takes a step back, waving off my worried look.

"Mom . . . ," I repeat.

"Go. Hurry, you don't have much time. You don't want to keep him waiting when he gets here."

"Don't you need to get back to Dad?" I ask hopefully.

"No, I'm having dinner with Miss Ina tonight at seven. I'm just going downstairs, so I have time to wait for your date to arrive before I head down to meet her."

I don't have time to ask her when she and Miss Ina became so close. I know I won't be able to convince her to leave, so I sigh.

"Fine. I'll be quick."

I go into the bedroom and shut the door. I left the outfit for tonight on my bed. Taking off my robe, I put on a pair of sheer black panties and a matching bra, then I grab my high-waisted blue jeans that are so tight I have a hard time getting them on. I pair them with a black long-sleeve, body-hugging top that I tuck into my jeans. I weave a black belt through the belt loops, fastening the fancy designer buckle before I sit on the edge of my bed. I zip on my thigh-high suede boots with the pointy toe and four-inch heels, then grab a long camel-colored sweater. I don't hear voices in the living room, so I go back into the bathroom to check myself out in the mirror.

I wonder what Antonio will think. I didn't want to dress up, because he doesn't seem like the kind of guy who would take me to a fancy restaurant. I still wanted to look put together and sexy, though.

I *do* look sexy, with my dark hair down around my shoulders in a mass of stylish waves, my makeup more dramatic than I wear it every day. I did a smoky eye and added false lashes to make my eyes pop even more. I added a light lip, lined and glossy. Nervousness starts to kick in, causing my heart to race. Tonight could either be the beginning of something that could be amazing or the end of my crush on Antonio.

God . . . I'm really hoping for the first.

Pulling in one breath after another, I take a step toward the mirror and look myself in the eyes.

"Libby Reed, you've gone on dates before. You know better than to get your hopes up," I whisper to my reflection before I turn off the light in the bathroom and walk through my bedroom.

I swing open my door to find Antonio standing just inside my living room, wearing a black peacoat over a beige sweater. The high collar accentuates his strong jaw. He's also sporting dark jeans that look great on him. And of course there are his ever-present boots. Seeing the amused smile that he's giving my mom, I wonder what she's been telling him.

"Sorry you had to wait," I say.

His head turns my way, and his eyes scan me from boots to hair before they lock with mine. The moment they do, the intensity I see there makes my stomach do a different kind of twist. The space between my legs tingles.

"Oh, honey, you look beautiful! Doesn't she look beautiful, Antonio?" Mom asks him with an elbow to his side.

I bite my lip.

"Yeah, Katie, she looks beautiful," he agrees quietly.

I wonder if my mom can feel the sudden charge in the air around us—a charge I feel every time I'm around him.

"Thank you."

I feel my cheeks get warm, and it takes everything in me to pull my eyes from him and look at my mom.

"You're supposed to meet Miss Ina, Mom . . . ," I remind her.

"Oh, right. I should do that and leave you two to your date."

She hurries to the couch to grab her things. I pick up my coat, only to have Antonio take it from me and hold it out. Turning my back to him, I slip it on. My eyes meet my mom's happy ones. I give my head a little shake, not wanting her to get her hopes up about this, but she just grins at me like the crazy woman she is.

"Antonio, it was so nice meeting you. You'll have to come out to Long Island with Libby sometime for dinner."

"Mom . . . ," I warn, but she ignores me and continues on.

"Or brunch. Really, whatever works around your schedule."

"Mom."

"I'd like that, Katie," he tells her.

I wonder if she told him to call her by her first name or if he just did that on his own.

"Well, then. It's settled. The next time you both have time, we'll plan for it," Mom says.

My jaw clenches. This must be what Mac and Fawn felt when Mom was all up in their business.

"Sounds good," Antonio agrees.

I grab my black slouchy leather bag with loads of tassels hanging from the seams and hook the strap over my shoulder.

"Good." Mom moves around me to give Antonio a hug, and I roll my eyes at the back of her head. I hold back a sigh when she turns to face me. "Call me when you get home."

"I'll call you tomorrow."

"Maybe I should just stay here tonight. You know . . . we can have a sleepover. That would be fun. We've never done that before."

Oh god.

"Mom, you need to get home to Dad. He would not be okay with you having a sleepover."

"He would be fine with it."

"When was the last time you slept in a bed without him?" I counter.

She looks up at the celling, trying to come up with an answer to that question.

"Right. Like I said . . . you need to get home to Dad after your dinner with Miss Ina."

"Fine. But you still need to call me tonight when you get home."

"Remember what we talked about earlier?" I ask quietly.

Her eyes narrow on mine, and she grits out, "Yes . . ."

"I'll call you *tomorrow*," I say, repeating my earlier statement.

"Fine. Call me tomorrow." She lets out a huff before putting a smile on her face that she aims at Antonio. "She can be a little hardheaded at times."

"Mom!"

"What?" She turns to look at me, and I glare at her. "It's the truth, honey. You're sweet as can be, but you really are hardheaded."

Hearing Antonio chuckle, I transfer my glare to him.

He grins at me.

Whatever.

"We should go," I mutter.

He wraps his fingers around mine, giving them a squeeze before opening the door.

"Love you," Mom says, stopping to kiss my cheek.

"I'm wondering if that's true," I grumble under my breath.

She smiles, then heads down the steps. Following her out, I wait until Antonio is out of my apartment before I lock the door and start down the steps with him at my back.

When we reach the first floor, he takes my hand. This startles me, and I look up at him.

"You really do look beautiful," he says.

"Thank you."

"And I really like your boots."

The roughly spoken compliment sends a shiver down my spine—and a different kind of shiver though my girlie bits.

"Uh . . . thanks," I repeat.

He shakes his head, smiling.

Hearing someone clear their throat, I look to the right and see Miss Ina and my mom waiting just inside of Miss Ina's apartment. They're both watching Antonio and me with completely opposite looks on their faces. Mom looks like she's watching a real-life movie star leading his woman down the red carpet at a Hollywood event, and Miss Ina looks like she's wishing she could rush across the space, snatch me from Antonio, take me into her apartment, and strap a chastity belt around me before throwing away the key.

"Have fun tonight, guys!" Mom calls out.

I fight the urge to roll my eyes at the overly chipper sound of her voice.

"Not *too* much fun, Libby Reed!" Miss Ina says.

Her eyes go to Antonio and narrow with a scary-old-lady look. Clearly, she would melt him into a puddle if she had that ability.

"Bye! Have a good dinner tonight."

I wave at them over my shoulder while I tug hard on Antonio's hand to get him to hurry up. I've already had to deal with him and my mom being in the same space—I don't want to know what Miss Ina might say if she has a chance to talk to him.

"In a hurry?" he asks, chuckling.

When we make it outside, I look up at him once. I notice that, even in my heels, he's still much, much taller than I am.

"You met my mom."

"I did." He smiles.

"That was bad—but not as bad as it could have been. Mom was on her best behavior."

"All right." His brows pull together slightly.

"Miss Ina is a wild card. If we had stopped to talk to her, she'd probably have demanded to chaperone dinner tonight—just so she can make sure I keep my virtue intact."

"I see."

His eyes change. Not in a bad way, but in a way that I don't exactly understand—until he turns toward me, rests his hands on my waist, and pulls our hips closer together.

"Your virtue *is* safe tonight," he says in a deep voice that makes my toes curl.

"I . . . Okay." I swallow.

"After tonight, all bets are off," he growls.

I feel the vibration of those words skim over me like thick honey. *Oh my god.*

My knees actually get weak, so I grab on to his jacket to keep standing upright.

"Antonio . . . ," I breathe.

"Fair warning." He bends his head and kisses the tip of my nose, then stands back and sticks out his arm into the street. A cab pulls up after half a second, and he opens the door and helps me in, then gets in with me.

I listen to him give the driver the address to the restaurant, and my eyes widen slightly. It's the same place where I had dinner with Walter.

"You okay?" he asks, pulling my attention to him.

"Fine." I try to smile at him, but his eyes narrow on my mouth.

"What is it?"

"Nothing." I keep my weird, awkward smile in place while I lace my fingers together in my lap to keep from twisting my hair.

"Have you been to Keens before?"

"I . . . Yes."

"Did that guy take you there?"

Staring at him, I wonder if I should lie about it. Then I figure I probably shouldn't.

"Yes . . . ?" I answer quietly, my admission sounding more like a question.

The muscles in his jaw jump, and he turns his head to look out the window. Leaning toward him, I rest my hand on his thigh. I try to ignore exactly how hard it feels under my palm. It takes a second for his eyes to come back to me, but when they do, I speak quietly.

"I kept thinking about you when I was at dinner with him," I admit for some stupid reason.

His eyes flare with surprise.

"I . . . I knew even before dinner was over that there would never be another date with him, no matter how nice he was. For some stupid reason, I've had a crush on you forever."

"What?" he whispers.

I wonder why the hell I just told him that, and why I didn't keep my big mouth shut—at least about the whole crush thing.

"Have a good night. I'm going to jump out of the cab into traffic now," I whisper back.

I start to look away, but before I can, his hand wraps around the side of my neck. Next, his fingers slide up into my hair, twisting it. Tingles shoot across my scalp as his mouth crashes down on mine. I gasp in surprise as his tongue thrusts between my parted lips and the familiar taste of him explodes on my tongue. Needing to keep myself here on Earth and not floating away, I clench my fingers into his sweater. I kiss him back, enjoy hearing him rumble when my tongue touches his.

God, I forgot how good it feels to kiss him, how good it felt when he nipped my lips and licked into my mouth.

I forgot how turned on he could make me with just his mouth on mine. Moaning, I slide one hand up his chest and latch on to his hair. I hear him groan in approval.

"Fuck, but you can kiss," he says as soon as he rips his mouth away and rests his forehead against mine.

"Ditto," I breathe as I pant, begging my lungs to fill with oxygen.

I slowly pull my eyes open to find him looking at me.

"So damn cute," he groans, closing his eyes and touching his lips to mine softly. "You're not jumping out of the cab, Libby. I don't give a fuck if that guy took you to Keens—we're having dinner there tonight since it should have been me taking you there in the first place."

He releases my hair, then wraps his arms around my waist and pulls me across the leather seat and deeper into his side. My stomach dances and my heart leaps. I've been called beautiful my whole life, so it no longer means anything to me. I know I'm pretty, but I've always wanted to be more than that to someone. So him telling me I'm cute is probably the sweetest thing he could have said. He also said that he should have been the one to take me to Keens, which I really hope means he would have wanted to take me even back then when I didn't think he liked me.

With a new kind of hopefulness in my chest, I sit close to him and try not to smile like an idiot—even though that's exactly what I want to do.

Once we arrive at the restaurant, he pays the cab driver and then helps me out of the back seat by taking my hand and keeping hold of it. When we get inside, he leads me through the crowd gathered near the door and over to the hostess. It's the same hostess who was here the night I had dinner with Walter. I wonder if she remembers me, then wonder if she remembers that I was here with a different man. Then I wonder if she thinks I'm a little bit loose for being here with two different men just weeks apart.

"I love your belt."

She startles me, and I come out of my head and focus on her. "And your boots. Did you get them from Nordstrom?"

"No, I found both online—secondhand," I admit.

"Really?" she breathes with wide eyes, like I just told her Santa Claus is real and he's going to drop off a bag of diamonds at her house tonight.

"Yeah. I . . . Do you want the website?"

"God, yes. I know that belt cost like four hundred dollars, and those shoes close to the same, so if I could get them for a discount, that would be awesome."

Okay, so she knows designers at a glance, which is impressive.

Feeling Antonio tense at my side, I wish she would stop saying how much my outfit cost retail—even if I didn't pay close to that for the belt or the boots.

"Do you have a pen I can use?"

She pulls one out from behind the stand and gives it to me along with a napkin.

I quickly write down the website and hand it back to her. "They get new stuff every week, so you just have to keep an eye out if you're looking for something specific."

"Awesome." She smiles, and I smile back.

"Reservation for Moretti," Antonio says in a tense voice.

Her eyes fly from mine to him and widen once more—this time with nervousness.

"Right. Sorry about that." She shoves the napkin into her pocket and then looks down at the iPad and does some clicking before grabbing menus. "If you'll follow me?" She smiles at us, then starts into the restaurant.

Antonio's hand settles into the small of my back as we walk, and I let out a relieved breath at his touch. It's starting to become crystal clear that he has an issue with money—or with money being spent on clothes and shoes. That probably doesn't bode well for us, since I *like* spending money on clothes and shoes. Then again, I work hard for the things I have. When we reach the back of the restaurant, I wonder if someone is playing some kind of twisted joke on me—it's the same table Walter and I sat at when we were here.

"Let me help you with that," Antonio says as I start to take off my coat.

I bite my lip as he slips it from my shoulders.

"Thanks."

"No problem."

He hangs it up on the hook near the table, then does the same with his own before pulling out the chair that's *not* facing the restaurant for me.

Once we're both seated, the hostess smiles at both of us as she sets down our menus on the table. "Your waiter will be with you shortly."

"Thank you." I give her a small smile, and she smiles back before taking off.

Looking around and nibbling my bottom lip, all I can think about is that I'm not sitting facing the restaurant.

"This isn't the good seat," I blurt out stupidly.

Antonio's eyes meet mine.

"What?" he questions, placing his napkin on his lap.

I sigh.

"I . . . well, everyone knows the good seat is the seat with the view of the restaurant." I wave my hand around the room.

"You're in the safe seat," he says.

I tip my head to the side in confusion and then ask, "The *safe* seat?"

"I have the view of the room. If something happens, I'll know first and will have time to get you to safety before anything can happen to you."

Holy crap.

"Oh," I mumble.

"Jesus, have you always been this cute?" he asks.

My chest starts to feel warm at his question.

"Um . . ."

"You have. Fuck me for being so stupid and not seeing it."

"Um . . . ," I repeat.

He smiles at me, then takes my napkin and hands it to me. I place it in my lap. We both order drinks when the waiter comes over. I have a glass of wine; he asks for a beer.

"I'm starving. I hope they actually have human-size portions of food at this place," he says, picking up the menu and looking at it when the waiter walks off.

"You haven't been here before?"

"No. Mom recommended it when I told her I was taking you out."

"What?" I feel my eyes grow to the size of saucers.

"I told her I was taking you out, and she said I should bring you here. She said that the food's good, that you'd like it."

"Your mom knows that we're out on a date?" I whisper.

"Yeah . . ."

"Oh my god," I keep whispering.

His smile turns into a grin.

"She's happy."

"I bet she is," I mutter.

He throws back his head and laughs—loud. Seeing him do it makes the warmth in my chest spread. I don't think I have ever seen him laugh that freely, so knowing I made him do it makes me want to do it again and again.

"I love your mom, but she can be just as bad as mine," I inform him as I pick up my glass of water and take a sip.

"Not sure about that, Princess," he says once his laughter has died down.

"I am."

"Babe, your mom doesn't know me from Jack who works at the corner store, but she invited me to come out to Long Island for dinner or brunch."

"This is true," I agree. "Then again, my mom knows that I had a crush on you."

"Had?"

"What?"

"Twice now you've said you *had* a crush on me. Past tense. Meaning you don't have one anymore," he explains.

"I . . . you . . . I . . . ," I stammer. "You've kind of been a jerk."

My softly spoken words taper off while the muscle in his jaw ticks. *Crap. Now why the hell did I say that?*

"Right," he says.

I look down at the menu in front of me, wishing we could go back in time a few minutes.

"I was an asshole," he says.

My head flies up, and our eyes lock. "I made assumptions I shouldn't have. I'm sorry about that," he says.

Seeing the honesty in his eyes, my body relaxes once more.

"It's okay."

"It's not okay. I won't do it again," he says firmly.

"What changed?" I ask, noticing that his eyes become intense when I do.

"I've wanted you from the moment I saw you, Libby. Fuck. I've imagined you in every position possible, but I wouldn't let myself go there because . . ." He runs a hand through his hair, looking away before looking back at me. "Those reasons are for another time. Not tonight. But like I said, I made assumptions, and I was wrong."

"Okay, but what changed?" I ask again.

What he just said makes it sound like all he wants is to sleep with me.

"Everything," he says.

Like that answers my question. It doesn't, so I blink at him.

"Everything?"

"There's a lot of things about you that I didn't notice until you started helping out at the shop."

"Oh," I say, feeling disappointed.

I drop my eyes to my menu.

"You're the hardest-working person I know." He grabs my hand. "You give all of yourself to everyone around you. You make each pizza like you're creating a piece of art. You're good to my parents and obviously good to yours and your sisters. You're sweet to the bone. Hell, even your neighbor looks like she wants to protect you from the world when she'd probably break a hip if she tried."

"Miss Ina is a wild card," I whisper, having nothing else to say. His words have rocked through me, throwing me off-balance.

"No, she cares about you. She wants to protect you from anything that might cause you harm. People like you are rare these days. Those who know how rare the qualities you have inside you are will always go to great lengths to protect them."

"I think you can stop talking now," I tell him, feeling so full of warmth from his sweet words that I'm afraid I might burst at the seams.

"I'll stop talking as soon as you tell me that you know I want more than to just fuck you."

"What?" I whisper as my mouth drops open in surprise at his crass words.

"I saw that look on your face, baby. I know exactly what you were thinking. Now I need you to tell me that you hear me when I say I want more than that from you."

"I hear you," I agree as my heart thunders away in my chest and my mind screams.

Please don't let this be too good to be true.

Chapter 8

FLUKE

LIBBY

"I heard you went on a date with Antonio last night?" Peggy says, coming into the back kitchen, where I'm stirring a pot of marinara sauce that has been cooking most of the day.

"I did."

I know there's no use trying to hide the smile that has been on my face since last night, when Antonio dropped me off at my door with a soft kiss and a promise to spend some time with me after we both get off work tonight.

"And . . . ?" she asks, leaning her hip against the counter at my side, crossing her arms over her chest, and raising one eyebrow.

"And we had dinner. It was nice," I answer vaguely, not wanting anything to get back to Martina.

"Just nice?" She frowns.

Dinner was beyond nice. I found out that Antonio can be more sweetheart than jerk when he wants to be. That he's easy to talk to and quick to laugh. That he's gentle and affectionate. Throughout dinner, he found reasons to touch me, to hold my hand or caress my face. After we left the restaurant, we walked with nowhere in mind. Then we stopped at a small café and shared a slice of chocolate cake. It was the perfect night, the perfect first date. Even the way he left me at my door with a soft kiss and nothing more was perfect.

"I had a great time."

"Okay, so are you going to go out with him again?" she asks.

"We have plans tonight," I admit. Her eyes light up. "You can't tell Martina," I add quickly when she starts to open her mouth. "I know you talk all the time, but I don't want her to know that we are seeing each other again. Not yet."

"Why not?"

"Because if things don't go well tonight, I don't want her to be disappointed."

"Why *wouldn't* things go well?" she asks, looking suddenly worried.

"Because last night could have been a fluke," I say, taking my eyes off her and going back to stirring the pot on the stove.

Like I said, last night was perfect. But nothing can stay perfect forever, which is why there is such a high demand for romantic movies and ice cream.

"Last night wasn't a fluke."

A deep voice I know all too well rumbles behind me, making me jump. I spin around to face Antonio, who had at some point stepped silently into the kitchen.

"You can tell my mom that Libby and I are spending time together tonight, and then again tomorrow, and the next day after that," he says, looking at Peggy.

"Antonio . . . !" I hiss.

His gaze snaps to mine.

"Are we not spending time together?" He crosses his arms over his chest.

"Well . . . yeah?"

It was news to me that we would be spending the next few days together—good news, but still news.

"Then she can know about it."

"I don't th—"

"I do." He cuts me off before I can tell him that I still don't think it's a good idea.

"Well, I think a customer just came in. I'm going to go check," Peggy lies before hurrying out of the back kitchen toward the front of the shop.

Antonio and I have a stare-down.

"I think we should talk about what we tell people about us," I say after a long moment.

He shakes his head and takes a step toward me. His hand comes up to wrap around the side of my neck. "We don't need to talk about it."

"I think we do."

I try not to be distracted by how good his hand feels on my neck, with his thumb sweeping softly against my pulse.

"If I didn't think we had staying power, I'd agree with you."

What?

"What?" I whisper aloud.

"You like me, right?"

"I . . ."

"You like me, and I like you."

"You *like* me?" I ask stupidly.

His head jerks back.

"Yeah."

"Oh."

"Fuck, but you're cute when you're clueless." He leans in to touch his mouth to mine quickly; then he pulls back, meeting my gaze once more. "Mom already knows we have plans tonight. I told her about them."

"You told your mom?"

"She's happy about the idea of me and you together. So yeah, I told her. She needs good stuff to think about right now."

"Oh my god," I whisper. "Why did you do that? What if things don't work out?"

"Did you call your mom today?" he questions, cutting me off. I look to the side. "Didn't you tell her we have plans tonight?"

"No," I admit.

He frowns.

"Why not?"

"My mom's crazy."

"What?"

"If I tell her we have plans tonight, she will likely call the nearest judge and ask when he can fit in a wedding. Then she'll toss out my birth control in hopes I get knocked up so you'll have a reason to stick around after we have a shotgun wedding."

"Baby . . ." His lips twitch like he thinks I'm being funny, and he shakes his head.

"You think I'm kidding, but I'm not." I rest my hands against his solid chest.

"You're on birth control?" he asks suddenly, changing the subject.

My body jolts.

"What?"

"You said she'd toss your birth control."

"I . . . well . . . yeah, I'm on birth control," I say, feeling my cheeks get warm at the admission of something so personal.

"Why?"

"Why?" I parrot.

"Yeah. Why are you on birth control?"

"Because . . ."

"Baby, you're a virgin. Why are you on birth control if you're a virgin?"

Oh my god. This conversation has suddenly gone completely past the point of embarrassing to humiliating.

"Do we really need to talk about this?" I question.

"Yeah," he answers firmly, bringing me closer to him by wrapping his hand around my hip.

"Okay. But do we really need to talk about this *right* now and *right* here?" I counter.

He looks around like he just realized where we are.

"Right. We'll talk about it tonight."

"Great. Something *not* to look forward to," I mutter.

He laughs, then leans down and touches his lips to mine before releasing me and taking a step back.

"Do you need help in here?"

"No, I've got it covered." I sigh.

"All right. I have some stuff to take care of in the office."

"Okay," I say, thinking that I should ask Martina and/or Tony to go over the administrative side of the business with me one day so that I will know what I'm doing when the time comes.

I know everything about running the front of the shop, but I'm clueless about everything that happens behind the scenes.

"It's just you and me closing tonight." He pulls me from my thoughts, and I focus on him. "Before we shut everything down, I'll make us a pie to take to your place."

"Sounds good," I agree.

He gives me a small smile, then leaves the kitchen.

Once I finish with the marinara sauce, I take it off the burner to cool. Then I grab the garbage and head to the back door. As soon as I step outside, a small flash of white zooms past me and disappears under the dumpster.

Living in New York, I'm used to rats. From the glimpse I caught, though, I thought it was a kitten. I grab my cell phone out of my pocket and turn on the flashlight, then lean down to see if I can see the cat. A pair of wide eyes stares back at me, and my heart melts in my chest.

I was right; it's a kitten. A tiny white one—or it looks like it once was white, but it's covered with grime and dirt.

"Come here, kitty, kitty," I whisper. It backs up. "I promise I won't hurt you." It takes a step toward me, then jumps back when a loud thud comes from somewhere close. "It's okay . . . There is nothing to be afraid of. I promise I won't hurt you." Seeing that my urging isn't going to bring him or her out of hiding, I head back inside. I wash my hands and then grab a paper plate and go to the front where we make the pizzas.

"Can you put some ham on here?" I ask Hector.

He looks at the plate, then at me. He shrugs before he places a few pieces of ham on the plate without question.

I go back outside and set the plate on the ground, then turn my flashlight back on the kitten and see that it's right where I left it.

"I brought you some food," I tell the kitten. It looks at me and then at the plate. I push it under the dumpster. "Come on, baby. It's okay."

It doesn't make a move toward the food. Figuring I will have to earn its trust, I leave the plate and head inside, hoping my absence will draw it out of hiding.

"What's going on?" Hector asks after I wash my hands again.

"There's a kitten outside under the dumpster. I was trying to lure it out of hiding with food."

"*Chiquita*, there's a million strays in the city," Hector says.

Antonio comes up to my side with a pen and paper in his hand.

"Why are you two talking about strays?" Antonio asks.

"Libby saw a stray cat out under the dumpster in the back."

"There's strays back there all the time, Princess."

I roll my eyes.

"I know, but this wasn't a cat—it was a kitten. A tiny, tiny kitten."

"You want to rescue it?" Antonio asks. I nod. "Baby, it's probably wild. Just call animal control."

"I will if I can't lure it out."

"If you can't lure it out?" he repeats, his brows pulling together.

"Yes."

"What are you going to do with it if you do manage to lure it out?"

I shrug. "I don't know. Give it a bath and take it home . . . ?"

"Take it *home*?"

"Why are you repeating everything I say?"

"Because you're talking about taking a feral cat home with you."

"It's just a kitten," I remind him.

"It's also wild."

"Whatever. I don't know why we're discussing this. I'm not asking you for help in luring it out or taking care of it."

"Taking care of it?" He looks at me like I have a few screws loose.

"Yes, taking care of it—*if* I can get it out. I'll take it home, clean it up, then take it to the vet to make sure it's okay."

"Then you're going to keep it?"

"Well, yeah, if I can."

"And if you can't keep it?"

"Then I will find it a good home."

"You're serious?"

He sounds surprised, and I really don't know why—I just told him what my plan was.

"I'm going to get my coat, then head down the block to the corner store to get some milk for it."

"Fuck me. You're serious."

"I already told you I was serious," I growl, and his face softens in a way that I have to say I like a whole lot.

"*I'll* go get you some milk."

"I can get it."

"And so can I. You stay here where it's warm. I'll go get you some milk for your wild cat," he says, making me wonder how it's possible that he can be a jerk and sweet at the exact same time.

"Whatever," I grumble.

He smiles at me before he takes off. I watch his ass in his jeans as he goes, thinking he really does have a great ass, great legs, a great back, and an awesome strut.

"It's about damn time," Hector mutters.

I swing around to look at him, realizing once again I was watching Antonio like a lovesick idiot in a romance movie.

"I'm happy for you two."

"I . . . Thanks," I mumble, ducking my head to hide the blush I know is covering my cheeks.

"Tony's told me and Marco about you buying the shop."

My stomach drops at this news, and my heart starts to pound.

"We hope you want us to stick around after everything is said and done."

"Yes," I whisper. "Of *course* I want you two to stick around."

"Good. We know not to talk about it with Antonio, though I don't get why you're keeping it from him."

"Um . . ." I bite my lip, not wanting to explain my reasons for not telling Antonio.

I know that I need to tell him about buying the shop before things between us go any further.

"It's your news to share, *chiquita*. We'll keep our mouths closed."

"Thank you."

"Anytime." He pats my shoulder before turning away from me and getting back to work.

Grabbing a rag, I clean off a table and work on talking myself into telling Antonio tonight that I'm buying his parents' business.

Chapter 9

Cold Pizza

Libby

"Where did it go?" I look around the alley for the kitten, who is no longer anywhere to be found. I searched for it earlier, when Antonio showed up with the milk for it, but didn't find it then, either.

"He's probably hanging with all the other strays—wherever they hang out," Antonio says from the back door of the pizzeria.

I glare at him over my shoulder, then start down the alley to see if I can spot the kitten hanging out around one of the other dumpsters.

"It's cold, Libby. You don't even have a coat on. Get your ass back in here."

"I know it's cold, Antonio. That's why I'm trying to find the kitten. It's a baby, and it's freezing. It could die out here."

"It's not going to die." He grabs my hand to prevent me from walking any farther down the dark alley. "We'll leave the milk out for him. With any luck, it'll get to it before the rats do."

"Aren't you just a ball of positivity?" I sigh.

He laughs as he wraps his arm around my shoulder to lead me back inside. I can't exactly spend my night tracking down the kitten, so I reluctantly let him lead me back inside the shop.

"You can try to catch your kitten again tomorrow," he tells me as he grabs the pizza he made for us to take to my place.

I glance at the back door, wondering if I should look one more time before we leave for the night.

"It'll be all right," he says, placing his fingers under my chin so I'll focus on him. "If you don't catch it by tomorrow, I'll call a friend of mine who does animal control for the city and have him come out to set a trap for you."

"Really?" I ask, swaying into him. His face softens.

"Yeah, Princess."

"Thank you."

He touches his lips to my forehead, then lets my chin go.

"Come on. Let's get our coats and go to your place."

He places a hand on the small of my back and starts leading me toward the office.

Nervous butterflies fill my stomach as I put on my coat and grab my bag. I didn't really have time to think about being alone with Antonio in my apartment earlier because of the distraction of work, the kitten, and then trying to come up with a way to tell Antonio about the shop. Now, with Antonio putting down the shutters and my place only a couple of blocks away, my mind is suddenly consumed by what could happen— and what I *want* to happen. I don't know that I'm ready to have sex, but I'm for sure ready to spend a lot of time making out with him.

"How are your sisters?" he asks, breaking into my thoughts as we walk toward my apartment hand in hand.

"They're good. Both of them have been pretty busy, so I haven't seen either of them for a while." I admit to myself that I'm a little upset about that.

"You guys are close, right?"

"There was a time when we were inseparable, but now I'm lucky to hear from them every other day," I say, knowing that I probably sound bitter. "Don't think I'm not happy for them—I am. I wish we could spend some time together."

"Maybe you should make plans with them," he says, giving my fingers a squeeze.

I shrug. "Maybe, but now that Fawn is married, I doubt she'll want to go out at night. And now that Mac is pregnant, I doubt she'd be up to going."

"What about lunch?"

"Maybe. Between my work most days at the salon, working on Designer Closet, and helping out at the pizzeria, my schedule is also kind of crazy right now."

"Designer Closet?" he asks.

I pause to glance at him, realizing that I've never told him about my side business.

"I rent items from other people's closets."

"You rent items out of people's closets?" he repeats.

I smile. He has the same look on his face that my dad had when I told him about my idea.

"Yeah. A designer dress can go for thousands of dollars, and most people can't afford to spend that kind of money on a dress they'll only wear once. That's where I come in. Let's say you have a ball to go to. You tell me your size, the kind of dress you're looking for, and I will hook you up. You pay a fee to me, and I give a percentage to the owner of the dress."

"Wow." He looks impressed, and I grin at him. "If you're too busy, you could always have your sisters stop by the shop. I'll make you guys a pizza. You can spend some time with them there."

"If Mac even catches a whiff of pizza, she'll be ready to puke, so I don't think that would go over too great with the other customers. But that's sweet of you to offer," I tell him as we head upstairs to my apartment. "Maybe I'll see if they want to catch a movie one day next week."

I let us into my place and turn on the light.

"My parents and I really appreciate you being at the shop and helping out, Princess, but the place won't fall apart if you don't come in every day," he tells me as he sets down the pizza on the counter in the kitchen.

I take off my coat.

"I know . . . ," I agree, turning away from him and thinking that this would be the perfect opening conversation for me to tell him why I've been working there so much.

"Fuck. If I didn't have to be there, I wouldn't be."

At his words, my stomach knots. I start to open my mouth, but before I can, his big body is in front of mine. When I see the heat in his eyes, that knot in my stomach shifts to tingles dancing between my legs.

"I need to tell you something," I say as he starts to shuffle me back toward the couch with his hands on my hips.

"Tell me."

"The pizzeria. I—"

"We're not talking about the pizzeria." He cuts me off as my knees hit the couch cushions.

"Antonio." I try again as he pushes me back.

I go down on the couch with him on top of me.

"We're *not* talking about the pizzeria," he repeats.

I stare into his eyes, then I watch his eyes drop to my mouth and darken.

"Okay, we won't talk about it."

He grins at me, sliding the back of his fingers along my cheek and into my hair.

"Been dying to get my mouth on yours all evening," he says right before he crushes his mouth to mine, making me forget about everything but him.

I lose myself in his kiss and his touch. I soak in every single detail in an attempt to memorize it, not wanting to forget any part. When he pulls his mouth away, I keep my eyes closed and pant while he does the same.

"You're really good at kissing," I blurt, then groan when I feel his body start to shake on top of mine with silent laughter. "Gahh. I think you short-circuit my brain. I can't seem to stop myself from telling you things I shouldn't be telling you."

"I like it," he says teasingly.

I open my eyes to look up at him.

"It's refreshing."

"It's also embarrassing."

"You shouldn't be embarrassed, Princess. I prefer you being overly honest to keeping shit from me."

My heart thumps hard. I open my mouth once more to tell him about the shop, then snap it closed when the next words leave his mouth.

"Now tell me—*why* are you on birth control?"

"I thought you forgot about that."

"How would I forget about it? We just spoke about it this evening." He frowns.

"Okay. Well, then, I thought you were going to let it go," I try.

He shakes his head. "I did let it go while we were at the shop. But we're not at the shop anymore."

"I'm hungry," I try again as I push at his chest to get him to move off me.

"You can eat in a minute." He denies me.

"I need to pee."

"You can pee in a minute," he says, wrapping his hands around my wrists and pulling them away from his chest, where I'm shoving uselessly.

"I can't wait to pee. I have a weak bladder," I lie.

He sits back slightly.

"Why don't you want to talk about it?"

"Because it's my business."

"If this is heading where I know it's heading, Libby, it's gonna be *my* business."

"Oh my god. You're so annoying. Get off me." I buck up against him, but he still doesn't move.

"Tell me what I want to know, and I will," he says.

My temper flares. "Fine," I huff, glaring at him. "My periods make me sick. That is, they used to until I got on birth control to regulate them. I would miss at least one day of work a month because I couldn't get out of bed the first day of my cycle. Now if I take a couple Advil and have a warm bath, that is usually enough to ease the pain," I finish. Then I ask snidely, "Are you happy now?"

"I'm not happy that you're in so much pain that you gotta miss work, but I'm happy to know so that if something like that happens, I can help you out," he says softly, running his fingers through my hair. "Don't be pissed at me for asking."

"I'm not pissed," I lie.

"I want to know everything about you, Libby. And I mean *everything*," he says, his voice tender.

"Do you think maybe we can start talking about that kind of stuff on . . . say . . . date number twelve?"

"No." He shakes his head, and I return to glaring at him.

"You know, you are seriously annoying."

"You've mentioned that before, Princess."

"Well, I don't want you to forget that, so I'll tell you again. You are annoying—*seriously* annoying."

"But you like me."

"I'm not sure about that anymore."

"Really?" He raises a brow. "Your tongue in my mouth and those sweet little sounds you were making a few minutes ago say differently."

"That was a few minutes ago."

"So if I kiss you now, you won't kiss me back?"

"Nope." I shake my head.

He grins, then lowers his mouth to mine, nipping my bottom lip.

"Kiss me," he coaxes, kissing my upper and then bottom lip before nibbling on them.

"No." I try not to give in. I really, really do. But when his hand moves up my side and his thumb sweeps under my breast, I lose all rational thought, open my mouth, and kiss him back.

"We need to stop," he says, pulling his mouth from mine sometime later.

Once more, it takes a few seconds for me to get my eyes to open. I shift under him, feeling the hard outline of his cock through his jeans and mine. I shiver.

"Yeah, we really need to stop," he mutters. But instead of stopping, he kisses me once more. This means by the time we do stop making out on my couch, we end up eating really cold pizza.

Still, I'm pretty sure it's the best pizza I've ever had.

∾

"Libby Reed, answer this door right now."

I force one eye open, then the other. I look at the clock next to my bed. Eight. Way too early to be up when I didn't get to sleep until after two, when Antonio left.

"Libby!" Miss Ina shouts once more, knocking—no, not knocking—*pounding* on the door.

"Go away," I groan, putting my pillow over my head in an attempt to drown her out.

"Answer this door," she shouts back, banging even more and using a hard object to do it.

Since I know she won't go away until I get up, I toss back the covers, roll out of bed, and stomp toward the door.

"Miss Ina, it's only eight in the morning," I snap as soon as I swing the door open. I find her with a cane in the air, ready to start pounding again.

"I know what time it is, child." She shoves past me into my apartment. "I waited until seven fifty-five to come up here because I knew it would take me a good five minutes to make it up the darn stairs to your door."

"You could have called me. I would have come down to you," I tell her, scrubbing my hands down my tired face.

"You would have ignored your phone until you finally got your behind out of bed."

She had me there—I would have.

"Okay, so what's so urgent?"

She narrows her eyes at me.

"Did that Antonio fellow come home with you last night and leave early this morning?" she asks.

"Since you know he was here last night and you were obviously spying on us, you know the answer to that question, Miss Ina." I sigh, moving toward the kitchen. I'll need coffee if I'm going to deal with her.

"I wasn't spying. I can hear everything that happens in this building—even the things I don't want to hear. Now answer my question."

"If I do, will you go away so I can get back to sleep?"

"No."

"I didn't think so," I mutter to myself, filling the coffeepot with water.

"You don't need to make coffee. We're going to have breakfast together after you tell me what happened last night."

"What?" I frown, my brain too tired to deal with her right now.

"I got breakfast in the oven downstairs. I made a casserole."

Oh lord. Why-oh-why did Mac befriend her, and why-oh-why did I think it was a good idea to do the same?

"Now tell me."

"Antonio came over last night."

"I know that part. Now tell me what happened," she snaps.

"We had pizza and watched a movie," I say, leaving out the fact that neither of us really watched the movie because our faces were glued together through most of it.

"That's all you did? Just watched a movie?"

"Yes, it was all very PG. Our clothes even stayed on the entire time."

It's a half truth, since I did lose my shirt at some point . . . but I kept my bra on.

"Hmm." She stares at me, and I stare back into her dark, almost-black eyes. I wonder if she can actually read what's written on my soul. "Good." She approves of whatever she sees. "Now put on some clothes and help me down the stairs. And hurry up about it. I'm hungry. I've been waiting forever on you to eat."

"You could have eaten without me," I inform her, leaving out the fact that since I didn't know we were going to be eating together this morning, it's not my fault she had to wait. "Never mind, I'll hurry." I hold up my hand when I see her eyes turn squinty; then I let out an exaggerated sigh. I leave the coffeepot as is and head for my bedroom.

I brush my teeth, wash my face, then put on a pair of sweats, a bra, and a hoodie. I shove my feet into a pair of slippers. Once I'm ready, I find Miss Ina sitting on the couch. She looks at me like I've made her wait a year rather than the maybe five minutes it took me to get dressed.

"Come on, old woman." I help her up from the couch, then down the stairs to her apartment. When we get inside, the smell of food makes my stomach growl. I smile at the table. "Did you mistakenly invite me instead of the queen?" I ask as she goes into the kitchen.

"No." She rolls her eyes at me, and I fight back a laugh. The table is set with fancy silverware, beautiful china, crystal cups filled with orange juice, and a gorgeous teapot with matching teacups.

"Sit down," she orders, bringing a casserole dish to the table and placing it on a trivet. She lifts the lid on another dish, and I see that she made toast.

"I'm starting to think you might like me, Miss Ina," I tell her as she takes two pieces of toast and places them on the plate in front of me.

"Don't get too excited. I promised your mom I'd find out what's going on with you and that boy. She said you're not telling her anything."

"You're bribing me with breakfast to get information for my mom?"

"She's worried about you," she grumbles, dishing out a large spoonful of cheesy potato, egg, and ham casserole onto my plate.

"I'm not telling her what's going on because, as of right now, there is nothing to tell."

"That boy leaving your place in the middle of the night says differently."

"We just watched a movie." I sigh.

"You said that already. Are you seeing him again?"

"Yes."

"When?"

"Today."

I shrug. We both work tonight, so he's asked me to come over to his place when we get off. I'm excited to see it—and even more excited to spend more time with him.

"This will be three dates in a row. I think that means you have news for your mom, don't you?"

"No," I answer, taking a bite of the casserole. "This is delicious, by the way."

"I know it is. I made it."

I smile around another forkful.

"How many times do you need to see this boy before you talk to your mom about him?"

"I don't know. Probably a million." I shrug, and she shakes her head. "Miss Ina, we're just getting to know each other. I don't want to talk to my mom about him until I feel more solid in what's happening between him and me."

"I don't understand you kids these days."

"Neither do I," I agree, picking up the glass of orange juice and taking a sip.

"Do you like him?" she prods after a few minutes of silence.

My stomach drops. I do like him—probably more than I should at this point. I'm also scared out of my mind.

"Well . . . ?" she prompts.

"I do like him."

"Then what's the issue?"

"I've had a crush on him for a long time."

"Your mom mentioned that." I'm sure my mom filled Miss Ina in on a *lot* of stuff when she was here for dinner the other night.

"I'm sure he's known that . . . Everyone else apparently did," I tell her, looking at my plate while pushing my food around. "And now, suddenly, he wants to spend time with me and is telling me he likes me. I just don't know if I'm ready to believe him."

"That's probably smart," she says softly. I lift my eyes to her. "It's probably smart to take things slow. If he really does like you, he'll wait for you to figure out your feelings."

"I hope so."

"If he doesn't, it's his loss. Not yours."

I'm not sure she's right. Now that I know how sweet Antonio can be, I'm starting to think it would totally be my loss.

Chapter 10

CUTE

ANTONIO

Arriving home from my morning run, I head down the hall to my kitchen and go right to the fridge. I grab a bottle of water, which I drain in a few gulps. When the front door buzzer goes off, I toss the empty bottle in the recycling bin and head to the door.

"Mom?" I frown, surprised to see her there.

"Hi, honey." She tips her head to the side so I can kiss her cheek.

"What are you doing here?" I ask, seeing that she's carrying several large shopping bags.

"Macy's is having a sale. I got you a new bedspread, sheets, and a few pillows," she says over her shoulder while walking into my apartment.

Staring at her back, I close the door and head down the short hall. She drops the bags on my brown leather couch, then starts to take off her coat.

"I don't need new sheets or a new bedspread." I walk into the kitchen to start a pot of coffee.

"Everyone needs new sheets every now and then." She hangs her coat on the back of one of the two wooden chairs that sits at my dining table, set between the kitchen and living room.

"If I needed them, I would buy them."

"Okay, then Libby will appreciate you having new sheets and a new bedspread when she comes over here." She rolls her eyes.

"What?" I frown as I scoop out coffee into the coffee maker.

"No woman wants to sleep on sheets that another woman has slept on, Antonio." She says it like I'm an idiot.

"No one but me has been in my bed or in my sheets since I moved into this place," I tell her.

Her eyes widen with surprise. "What?"

"I'm not talking about that part of my life with you."

Really, I have no idea why I even mentioned it. The fucked-up truth is that it didn't seem right to bang some other chick while thinking about Libby—and I've been thinking about Libby since the moment I met her.

"You haven't—"

"Mom, I'm never going there with you. So drop it," I growl.

She presses her lips together, then mutters, "I just can't believe this."

"Jesus."

"Antonio Enzo Moretti, do not use the lord's name in vain," she snaps, shooting daggers at me while crossing herself.

"Take the stuff you bought back to the store. I don't need it," I say, getting back to the conversation at hand.

"I'm not taking them back. I bought them for you. Plus, I got a great deal." She pulls out a set of sheets that are covered in flowers. Bright, colorful fucking *flowers*. Then she pulls out a comforter covered with the same floral pattern.

What the hell?

"Seriously?" I look from the sheets, comforter, and throw pillows my mom is setting on the couch to her.

"Aren't they pretty?" She picks up one of the bright-pink pillows—which is also in the shape of a flower.

"Take them back," I demand, grabbing two mugs out of the cupboard.

"Libby will like them."

"Libby doesn't live with me."

"She might one day."

I look over at her. Libby was right. We should have kept things just between us for a while. I didn't only because, with all the bad shit coming at my mom, I wanted her to have something good to think about. I'm starting to see the error of my ways.

"Maybe, but that day isn't today."

"I was just trying to help," she says, sounding dejected. She comes into the kitchen, and I sigh as I give her a hug. "Do you like her?" She tips her head back to look up at me.

I feel my gut get uncomfortably tight but push past it to answer, "Yeah."

She nods. "She's a good girl."

"She is," I agree.

I didn't know it before. I *couldn't* have known it before because I didn't even try to find out. But now I know she's a good woman, a sweet woman, a hardworking woman.

Yeah, I like her . . . maybe too much.

"I hope it works out between you two. I want a grandbaby."

I look up at the ceiling.

"Can I date her for a month before you and her mom start working on getting grandchildren out of us?"

"It sounds like I should meet her mom."

"That's not going to happen."

"Why not?" She shoves my chest playfully.

"Because you are bad enough on your own. If you had someone to plot with, you'd be out of control."

"You aren't getting any younger, Antonio."

"I think I got a while before I need to start worrying about my age affecting my ability to father children."

"A while?" she repeats.

"A while," I concur, laughing when her eyes fill with disappointment.

Yeah, Libby was right. I should have kept my mouth shut.

～

Taking the garbage out at the restaurant, I stop and then stare at the small kitten whose face is in the bowl of milk Libby put out earlier in the evening. When the kitten finally notices me, his head—I decide it's a "he" for some reason—comes up out of the bowl. He blinks his bright-blue eyes. Even covered in grime, the little guy is cute.

"Hey, buddy." I get down on my haunches, and he backs up a step. "It's okay." I slowly stick out my hand toward him. "I won't hurt you." He takes one step toward me, and then another and another until his cold wet nose is pressed against the tips of my fingers. "You're kind of cute." I let him sniff my fingertips before I run my index finger up the bridge of his nose to the top of his head. His back arches, and I grin and slide my fingers along his back. "Do you think you'd let me pick you up without biting the shit out of me?" I ask him as he rubs his face against my hand, forcing me to pet him. "You're gonna make my girl happy. I think you might just gain me some ground with her." I carefully scoop him up. I expect him to start hissing, biting, and scratching, but instead he looks up at me and blinks again. He tilts his head to the side. Smiling, I pick up the trash and drop it in the dumpster, then take him through the back door and head for the office—I know Libby is there. When I get there, I find her putting on her coat. "Got a surprise for you," I say.

Her eyes are drawn to my chest, where the kitten is resting in one of my palms.

"Oh my god." She comes toward me slowly. "How did you catch him?"

"He was drinking the milk you left out. He didn't run when he saw me."

She takes another step, then slowly reaches out her hand toward the kitten and touches one finger to the top of his head.

"Did he bite you or anything?" She looks up at me, but I shake my head no. "So he's not wild."

"I didn't say that, Princess," I murmur.

She grins, then drops her eyes back to the kitten and starts petting him once more.

"You are so cute, Mr. Blue Eyes," she murmurs, rubbing him behind his tiny ears. "You're also really dirty." Her nose scrunches up.

"We'll give him a bath at my place."

"We need to get him some food."

"We can stop at the corner store on the way."

"Do you want me to hold him while you get on your coat?" she asks hopefully.

I laugh. "Yeah." I transfer him over to her and smile when he doesn't put up a fight. "What are you going to name him?"

"I don't know. I don't know if it's a boy or a girl." She holds him up to her face so she can look into his eyes. "Are you a boy?" she asks. The kitten tips his head to the side. "Or are you a girl?" The kitten blinks, then lifts its paw and swipes at her nose.

"I think he's a boy, baby."

"Why do you think that?" she asks, looking at me.

"Because he's got balls."

"He does?" She lifts him up to look at the underside of his belly. "Oh. Well, then, how about we name him Catsanova?"

"Catsanova?" I repeat, zipping up my coat and smiling.

"Yeah."

"Try again." I shake my head.

"Catzilla?"

I shake my head again.

"JustKitten, Kit Kat, Purrfect, Santa Claws, Catsup, Catillac?"

"Have you been thinking of these names for a while?" I ask, laughing at her.

She grins at me. "I googled funny cat names a while back, when I was thinking about getting a cat for myself."

"I see." I lead her out of the office, then out the front door. I lock it behind us.

"What do *you* think we should name him?" she asks me as I put the key in the lockbox and close the shutters.

"Pool," I answer. She looks at me, confused. "His eyes are blue—the color of a pool."

"I like it." She smiles, then holds up the cat again.

For a wild kitten, he's pretty damn okay with all this attention.

"What do you think, Pool?" she asks. The cat takes another swipe at her nose. "Good. Glad you like it." She tucks the cat back against her chest.

"Come on." I lead her across the street to the corner store, where I pick up a few cans of wet cat food along with litter and some stuff for breakfast in the morning before getting us into a cab to go to my place. Libby doesn't know it yet, but she *will* be spending the night with me tonight. I wanted to stay with her last night, but when I saw that she slept on a twin-size bed, I knew that would be impossible. I haven't slept on a twin-size mattress since I was in middle school. I'm sure I could have found a few creative ways to make us both fit in her bed, but I also know she's not ready for the ways I'd do that.

Honestly, I don't know if I'm ready, either. Do I want Libby? Yes, but knowing she's a virgin, I want to make sure we have a strong foundation before we take our relationship to the next level. I don't want to sleep with her, take a gift that she can only give away once, then have things go bad between us. Then again, the idea of another man taking her virginity makes my stomach twist with vicious jealousy.

"Are you okay?"

Hearing her softly spoken question, I focus on her again. "Yeah, Princess."

"You seemed far away."

"Just thinking." I slide a chunk of her hair off her shoulder and run my fingers through it.

"Are you sure?" she asks as the cab pulls to a stop in front of my building.

"I'm sure," I say before I pay the cab and help her out of the back seat.

"This is nice." She looks around, and I follow her gaze up and down my quiet block.

I've lived in the Riverdale section of the Bronx for the last two years. It's a quiet area with a small-town feel, even though it's just fifteen minutes from Manhattan. I chose this part of the city because I need calm after working in the city for days at a time. I love my job, but it's high stress. Having the quiet of this place to come home to helps me unwind. Plus, people know me. Everyone knows everyone. If you go to breakfast at the local café, they will ask you your name and then call you by it each time you come in. It's refreshing after living in the city for so long and just being another face.

"Come on. Let's get Pool inside, cleaned up, and fed." I lead her to the front door; it opens as if automatically when we reach it.

"How's it going, Antonio?" Carson, the doorman, asks when Libby and I walk into the lobby of the building.

"Going all right. Did I get any packages?"

"Nope, not today," he answers. His eyes go to Libby, and he smiles before turning his attention back to whatever it is he was doing before we walked in.

"This is a nice building," Libby says as we get on the elevator.

I hit the button for my floor, then wrap my hand around her hip and bring her closer to me.

Petting the top of the kitten's head that's tucked between us, I agree. "It is. It's also a lot cheaper living here than the city."

"Is it?"

"Yeah. I had a one-bedroom shithole on the West Side before moving here, and my rent was triple what it is now."

"Living in the city *is* expensive."

"It is." I slide my hand down to rest on her lower back and lead her off the elevator.

My apartment is at the end of a long hall. Pulling out my key, I unlock the door and let us both inside. I set down the bag with the cat food and groceries on the kitchen counter.

"I didn't even ask if you have stuff we can use to give him a bath," she says as I empty the shopping bags and finish putting things away.

"I have some shampoo we can use tonight. Anything else he'll need we can get tomorrow." I gather an old towel from the linen closet and a bottle of shampoo from my shower, then go back to the kitchen. Libby is still standing with Pool in her arms—now without her coat on.

"I don't think he's going to like this very much," Libby says as I turn on the water to fill the sink.

"Probably not," I agree. "But he needs a bath all the same."

"Okay, Pool. You've been a very good kitty, so please don't bite us now," Libby says, handing him over to me once I have the sink half-full.

I carefully take Pool from her and place him in the sink. He starts to freak out. He doesn't bite, hiss, or scratch, but he does everything in his power to escape the sink—and us.

"This is fun," Libby says.

I look at her and laugh when I see how wet she is. Her shirt is soaked through, and even some of her hair is wet.

"This isn't exactly what I would call fun, baby," I tell her as I haul Pool back under the water to rinse the second round of shampoo from his fur.

"Well, at least he didn't bite us," she murmurs, grabbing the towel from the counter and holding it out so I can hand her Pool.

He has a "pissed kitty" pout on his face.

"See? You're all done. I bet you feel better, don't you?" she asks Pool.

He untucks one of his paws from the towel and bats at her chin.

"Leave him to roam, baby. Let's get you something dry to wear," I tell her.

Her eyes meet mine, and she looks around the room.

"What if he gets lost?"

"This place is less than a thousand square feet. We'll find him."

I take Pool from her and set him on the ground, then take her hand. I lead her into my bedroom and flip on the light, then go to the dresser and grab T-shirts for both of us. When I turn around, I find her bent over and taking off her boots.

My eyes automatically zero in on her heart-shaped ass. Silently telling my cock to calm the fuck down, I hand her one of the T-shirts.

"My jeans are soaked, too," she tells me with a smile.

I go back to my dresser and grab a pair of sweats that will be way too big for her and hand them to her as well. I expect her to ask to use the bathroom, so when she takes off her top right there and drops it to the floor, my mouth goes dry and my feet lead me right to her. The bra she has on is black lace, sexy as hell. I pull her toward me, meeting her gaze.

"Do you know how perfect you are?" I ask.

Her face gets soft while her hands move to rest against my chest.

"You're pretty perfect, too, you know," she says.

I lower my mouth to hers and kiss her softly. Her hands slide up under my shirt, and she pushes it up until it's over my head. She presses her bra-covered chest into me as she gets up on tiptoe to deepen the kiss.

"We need to slow down," I tell her as her nails scrape down over my pecs and abs.

"I know," she agrees, shoving me backward.

I fall onto my bed, and she comes down on top of me.

Her mouth hits mine as soon as we land.

"Fuck, but I want you." I flip her to her back, then lick and nip her neck, and then the edge of her breast. I enjoy listening to the sounds she's making.

"Antonio, please touch me," she begs, raising her hips.

My jaw clenches, and I fight an internal battle with myself as I stare into her beautiful need-filled eyes.

"Please."

"Fuck it."

I deftly unhook her bra and slide it from her shoulders, then unsnap her jeans and pull down the zipper. She raises her hips off the bed and helps me pull her jeans down, then kicks them off. I waste no time positioning myself between her legs when she spreads them open for me. I slide my hands under her ass and lift her into my mouth. The first taste of her on my tongue is enough to send me into a frenzy. Licking, nipping, sucking, biting—I eat her like a man famished. Her nails dig into my scalp, and her fingers pull my hair as she grinds herself against me. Carefully, I slide one finger inside her. Her hips buck up off the bed, sending her deeper into my mouth. Feeling her start to convulse around my finger, I pull her clit into my mouth and suck. Her body stills and her back arches as she comes hard. Fuck, but hearing her and seeing her come is enough to push me close to the edge. Resting my forehead against her pelvic bone, I pull in a few much-needed deep breaths to try and get myself under control.

"I think I just saw the light," she whispers.

I smile.

"Maybe I actually died," she continues.

I laugh, looking up at her body. Her eyes are closed and her cheeks are flushed. She looks beautiful, so damn beautiful.

"You're staying the night," I inform her.

Her eyes open and her chin dips so she can look at me.

"You're staying the night," I repeat when our eyes lock.

"I . . ." Worry fills her eyes.

I slowly slide my finger out of her, listening to her gasp as I do, then move up her body until I'm over her and looking down into her sated eyes.

"Baby, we're not going there. Not yet. You'll tell me when you're ready for that. I just want to hold you tonight."

"Really?"

"Really." I run my fingers down the side of her face.

"Okay," she whispers. "I'll stay the night."

"Good." I kiss her forehead, then lean back to look at her once more. "You feeling okay?"

"Yeah." She lifts her hand to touch my jaw.

"Good." I lean down and kiss her softly once more. "That was beautiful, baby. Probably the most beautiful thing I've ever experienced."

Her eyes warm.

Fuck, seeing that look of contentment in her eyes . . . I know I could easily fall in love with her.

"I don't know if I should say thank you or not."

I start to laugh. "No thanks necessary." I smile. "It was my pleasure." Her cheeks get dark, and I laugh again. "We should probably get up and check on Pool."

"What about y—"

"I'm good." I cut her off, knowing what she's going to ask. I don't have the ability to think about that right now. Not with her still naked, her cheeks still flushed, the scent of her sex still in my nostrils, and the taste of her on my tongue.

"But . . ."

"I'm good." I squeeze her waist and then kiss her once more before I help her up off the bed. Looking down at her once she's on her feet, I grin. "You're short without your heels."

"I'll always be short compared to you," she tells me as she smiles. "It's nice not having to worry about how high my heels are when I'm with you."

"You worried about that before?"

"Well, if I had a date with a guy who was short or just as tall as me, I couldn't wear whatever heels I wanted to—I had to be considerate of his emotional vulnerability about his height," she says.

I toss my head back, laughing.

"Glad you don't have to think about that when you're with me, baby." I kiss the tip of her nose and then let her go so I can hand her the shirt I gave her earlier. As much as I love looking at her beautiful body, there is no way I will be able to keep control over myself if she doesn't put something on. "You get dressed. I'm going to see if I can find Pool. I'll give him some food, then I'll find *us* something to eat while we watch a movie."

"Do you have popcorn?" she asks.

I think for a minute, then shake my head no. "Darn. Okay, I'll go out as soon as I get dressed."

I grab my shirt and put it on, then leave her in my bedroom. When I reach the living room, I find Pool lying on the couch. When he sees me, he jumps down and follows me into the kitchen. I grab an old cake pan from the drawer under the stove and fill it with cat litter, then set it down. I make a mental note to get a litter box tomorrow. I then dump a can of cat food into a bowl and set it down, along with a bowl of water. Pool sniffs the cat litter and then goes to the food and starts to scarf it down.

Libby comes out of my room wearing my shirt and my sweats, which make her look adorable.

"You better come kiss me before you mess with Pool," I tell her.

She grins at me, stopping in her tracks. Once she's close, she touches her lips to mine.

"Better?"

I stare into her eyes. "Yeah, baby," I tell her, knowing she has no idea just how much better I am.

"Good." She goes to Pool while I search for something for us to snack on.

Finding some crackers in the cupboard—and not much else—I go to the freezer and grab a bag of fries made out of broccoli and potatoes, then turn on the oven.

"I take it you're not a fan of junk food," she says as she watches me dump some fries onto a baking pan and place it in the oven.

"With what I do, I try to stay in shape. Part of me staying in shape is putting good things in my body. So, no, I don't eat a lot of junk food."

She nods.

"What about you?"

"You saw my feast a few weeks ago when you came to my apartment."

I did see her feast: chips, candy, takeout. I don't mind eating crap food every now and then, but I don't do it often.

"I like junk food."

"Do you work out?" I ask.

She cringes. "No, I think I'm allergic."

"Sorry, Princess, but no one's allergic to working out."

"That's what you think. I sweat and get all red and blotchy—I'm pretty sure that's an allergic reaction."

Laughing hard, I hook her around the waist and pull her toward me. "That's just what happens when you work out."

"Okay . . . ," she agrees, dropping her eyes to my mouth.

"You get sweaty and red during sex, too, baby. And even if you are allergic to *that*, you're gonna have to get over it because I plan on getting you all sweaty and red a lot."

"Oh . . . ," she breathes.

I touch my mouth to hers, then lean back, smiling. "God, you're cute."

Her lips part, and her body melts into mine.

"I like that you think I'm cute," she whispers, sliding her hands up my chest.

"Yeah?"

"Yeah."

"You *are* cute—and you're sweet."

"I'm glad you think that, too," she says.

I shake my head. Most women want to be told they're beautiful, sexy, or hot. But then there's Libby, happy with being told she's cute.

Not just happy—I can tell the way her face gets soft every time I say it that it means a lot more to her.

"What movie do you want to watch?"

"What do you have?"

I open the cupboard under the TV where I keep my DVDs.

"You like scary movies, too!" she says.

I grin at her as she gets down on her knees and starts to go through them.

"My dad took me to see the movie *It* when it was playing in Times Square when I was a kid. I was freaked out of my mind for a whole week after watching it, but I wanted to see it again and again. After that, I became obsessed with scary movies," I tell her as her eyes meet mine.

"Seriously?" she asks.

"Seriously what?"

"That was my first scary movie, too."

"Really?"

"Yeah, I love that movie. I still watch it every now and then, but it's not as scary as it was the first time I saw it." She smiles, then goes back to looking through my collection.

She holds up a movie and picks up Pool when he wanders over to her. Tucking him under her chin, she kisses the top of his head while I put the movie into the DVR player. We settle in on the couch. When the fries are done, Libby adds cheese to the top of hers. We eat on my couch while we watch *The Blair Witch Project*.

When the movie comes to an end, we get Pool to use the litter, then we both brush our teeth in my bathroom, side by side, before getting into bed.

"Antonio?" Libby says quietly.

I give her hip a squeeze.

"Yeah, Princess?" I ask when she doesn't say more.

"You work tomorrow night at the fire station, right?" she asks softly.

I look down at her in the dark, not really able to see her facial expression.

"Yeah, tomorrow and the night after. Then I'll have a couple more nights off. What's up?"

"Your job isn't exactly safe," she says quietly.

My gut tightens.

"I—"

"My job's *not* safe, Libby." I cut her off and pull her up my body until her face is closer to mine. "*Life* isn't safe. Nothing is guaranteed, baby. That's why you need to appreciate every single moment. That said, I work with good people who have my back. I might not be safe . . . but I'm as safe as I can be."

"Okay," she whispers, resting her hand on the side of my neck. "I . . . I just want you to know that you shouldn't do anything crazy like run into a burning building to rescue a cat. I might miss you if something happened and you didn't make it back out."

Fuck.

My arms tighten around her. Aside from my parents, no one else has cared about me in a long fucking time. It feels good. Really fucking good.

"I won't run into any burning buildings to rescue a cat," I tell her gruffly.

"Good." She settles into my side, then I feel her lips touch lightly against my pec. "Night, Antonio."

"Night, Princess."

I roll toward her so that we are facing each other, toss my leg over hers, and wrap her up in my arms. I feel Pool, who is lying on the bed at our feet, get up and move around before settling back in. I don't know how long I stay awake holding her, but I do know it takes me a while to find sleep. All I can think is, I should have opened my fucking eyes sooner and seen what was right in front of me. If I had, I could have had this all along.

Chapter 11

It Feels a Lot Like . . . Like

Libby

"Mom, we're here!" I shout as I walk into my parents' house. Miss Ina, who came with me for dinner, gives me an unhappy look. "What?"

"It's rude for a young woman to shout."

"I'm in the kitchen!" Mom shouts.

I grin at Miss Ina, who rolls her eyes. I drop my purse on top of the small table near the front door, then take off my coat and hang it in the coat closet.

I start to help Miss Ina with her coat, but I have to back away from her when she starts to slap at my hands. "Stop fussing over me all the darn time," she says crankily.

"I was just trying to help you out," I say, hiding my smile when she glares at me. I don't know what it is, but I really like annoying the woman. It's becoming my favorite pastime.

"Was there a lot of traffic?" Mom asks as we walk into the kitchen. It's where she likes to spend most of her time. She's always puttering around the kitchen making something, sitting at the island writing out lists, or chatting online with her friends on her laptop.

"Yes," Miss Ina answers.

Simultaneously, I answer, "No."

"I see." Mom smiles, looking between the two of us. "Now tell me again why you couldn't invite your boyfriend to come along with you?"

"He's working the next two days," I say, reminding her of exactly what I told her on the phone that very afternoon, when she asked me to come out to Long Island to have dinner with her and my dad.

"How are things going between you two?"

I shrug my shoulders.

"She didn't come home last night. I'd say they're going okay," Miss Ina informs my mom.

I look down at her and narrow my eyes. "Will you stop spying on me?" I snap at her.

She smirks.

"You didn't sleep at home last night?" Mom whispers.

I grit my teeth. "I stayed at Antonio's place."

"Was it PG?" Miss Ina questions.

I don't look at her again. "Yes. Very, very PG," I lie outright.

What we did before we watched a movie was not very PG at all, and what we did when he woke me up this morning was a whole lot less PG than that. It was also amazing. Still, even with how amazing the orgasms were, going to sleep in his arms and waking up with him was the best part of the whole night.

"You look like you're in love. Are you in love?" Mom asks hopefully.

My stomach drops.

Am I in love? I don't think so, but I've never been in love before so I don't know what it feels like. "Ugh," I answer lamely.

"I think it's love," Miss Ina contributes, going around the island to stand next to Mom, across from where I've taken a seat on one of the three barstools at the counter.

"I think right now that I'm in *like* with him."

"In *like* with him?" Mom frowns, looking confused.

"It feels a lot like . . . like," I say, nodding my head.

Mom looks at Miss Ina. "Do you know what being 'in like' means?"

"I don't think it means spending the night together," she says.

I sigh. "Can we not talk about that right now?"

"You're starting to be as closed up as your sisters are about their relationships," Mom says, sounding disappointed.

"When there is something for you to know, you will be the first person I tell, Mom. But as of right now, Antonio and I are just seeing each other. I don't know what will happen between us, and I'm trying not to think too much about it. I like him and I think he likes me—right now that's all I know."

"I guess," she grumbles, turning to stir whatever she's cooking on the stove.

"Mom . . . ," I groan. She looks at me. "You have a new son-in-law and a grandbaby coming. You should be happy with that."

"I am happy, but I want all my girls happy and settled."

"I'm happy, Mom. Really happy," I say gently.

Her face softens. "Okay," she whispers.

"Okay," I whisper back.

"Now tell me about Pool," she says.

I smile. This morning Antonio went with me to the vet, who said Pool is in perfect health for a stray. When we left the vet, he took me to the pet store to get all the things I would need, like a litter box, food, a collar, and some toys. I told Mom about Pool when she called to invite me to dinner. Okay, she didn't actually *invite* me . . . she *told* me I'd better be there and that I needed to bring Miss Ina to get her out of her apartment.

"He's adorable. I wanted to bring him with me, but I figured it would be better to leave him to get used to his new place."

"What are you two talking about?" Miss Ina looks between Mom and me.

"I got a kitten," I tell her.

She frowns at me. "Cats aren't allowed in the building."

"How will the landlord know if I don't tell him?" I ask.

Her brows pull sharply together as she answers. "*I* am the landlord, child, and you just told me about it."

"You're not the landlord."

"Yes, I am," she says so vehemently that I know she's not lying.

"You are?"

"Yes. My husband and I bought that house right after we were married."

"But I pay rent to an agency."

"I don't have time to deal with all the issues that come with being a landlord, so I hired out," she informs me, waving her hand around. "And I don't allow animals in my building."

"So you're going to make me move because I have a cat?" I ask her. She frowns. "What if I give you a pet deposit?"

"Why did you get a cat when you know they are not allowed in the building?"

"I didn't go to a store and buy him, or even adopt him from the pound. I saw him behind the pizzeria in the alley a couple nights ago. I tried to rescue him then, but he disappeared. Last night Antonio caught him, so we took him to his place and got him cleaned up. This morning I took him to the vet to make sure he was okay. He is, so I brought him home."

"So he's a *wild* cat?" she says, sounding disturbed.

"He's just a kitten. He's actually really sweet. He didn't even try to bite or scratch me or Antonio when we gave him a bath."

"If Miss Ina won't allow you to keep him, you can bring him here. Your dad and I will take him," Mom says.

Disappointment fills my stomach. I don't want to get rid of him. I've already fallen in love with the little guy. It was nice having another living being in the apartment with me when I was home today. Plus, he followed me around everywhere, even when I was doing my makeup and hair. He sat right there on the closed seat of the toilet, watching me.

"Miss Ina, please don't make me give him away," I beg. I swear I see her expression warm. "Please? I promise I will make sure that he doesn't do anything to destroy the apartment. I will pay whatever pet deposit you want me to."

"All right, child. Stop begging. You can keep the cat," she acquiesces with a dismissive wave.

I quickly scoot off my stool and wrap her up in a tight hug. "Thank you." I jump up and down, keeping hold of her.

"Stop hugging me. You're wrinkling my clothes," she complains, trying to shove me off. I don't budge. I hug her tighter. Finally, she lets her arms fall to her sides and gives in to my embrace. Smiling, I kiss the top of her head quickly. Then I let her go and duck when she tries to smack me.

"You really do like me, don't you, Miss Ina?" I grin as she swipes her hands down the front of her top and pants. Then her eyes meet mine, and she glares.

"Don't make me change my mind."

"You *do* like me. I think I might hug you again," I tell her, listening to Mom laugh.

"What's going on in here?" Dad walks into the kitchen, and I wrap my arms around his waist. I feel his lips touch the top of my head as he gives me a hug. "Hey, honey."

"Hey, Dad." I look up at him, and he smiles.

"You want a beer?" Mom asks him. He nods, wrapping an arm around my shoulders and pulling me into his side.

"How are things going with the pizzeria?" he asks me.

"Good. We're getting closer. We should close in a couple weeks if everything goes as planned. I'll let you know a few days or so in advance so you can schedule the time off to be there when it's time to sign the papers."

"Good." He grins at me.

"Have you thought of a name yet?" Mom asks.

"Princess Pizza," I say, and she laughs. "I'm serious. I already started the designs for the logo, and I plan on closing down the shop for a week and having some changes made to the interior after we sign the papers."

"What kind of changes?" Miss Ina asks.

"There's a large storage room in the back of the shop that I want to have gutted. I plan on making it a space that's available for rent. Parents can rent it for a birthday party, for example, or they can get a package where the kids will be able to make their own pizzas in there."

"That's actually a really great idea," Mom says with a proud smile.

"I'm excited. Scared, but really excited about it."

"We're proud of you," Dad says.

I tip my head back to smile up at him, and he gives my shoulder a squeeze.

"Have you told Antonio?" Mom asks. I shake my head, hating the disappointment I see in her eyes. "Honey, you need to tell him."

"I know. I'm going to tell him when I see him next."

"I think you should tell him before that," Dad urges. Miss Ina nods her head.

"He's working the next two days. It's not something I want to share with him over the phone, but I do plan on telling him as soon as I see him again."

"I hope you know what you're doing," Mom says quietly.

Fear fills my stomach and chest. I have *no* idea what I'm doing. I should have told him after our first date, but I stupidly didn't. Every time I've tried to tell him since then, I've gotten distracted by his kisses and touches. Or he's completely shut me down when I've brought up the shop.

"It will be okay. He'll understand why I didn't tell him before," I say, hoping that uttering those words out loud will make them true.

"Okay . . . ," Mom agrees reluctantly.

"Do you want me to set the table?" I ask, needing something to do. She nods.

I give my dad's waist a squeeze, then let him go so I can set the table. I help Mom put out the food. After dinner, Miss Ina insists that we catch a cab back into the city, and I make it to the shop in time to help Hector close down the pizzeria.

~

"Hello?" I answer my cell phone, bringing it under the covers with me. I got into bed a while ago. Even though I'm beyond tired, I have had a hard time finding sleep.

"Hey, baby."

Antonio.

"Hey," I say, feeling my stomach get warm. "Is everything okay?"

"Everything's fine. Just missed the sound of your voice."

Oh my god.

"You did?"

"Yeah," he says.

I can hear the smile in his voice. I've missed the sound of his voice, too, which is ridiculous since it's only been a day since I've heard it. Actually, if I'm being honest, I miss him.

"I miss you . . . I mean . . . . I . . . uh . . ."

"It's okay." He laughs, but I groan and cover my face with my hand. "Good to know I don't even have to be in the same room with you to short-circuit your brain."

"I don't know that that's a good thing," I mumble, feeling Pool walk up my body and then stop on my chest. Opening my eyes, I see him in the dark, staring at me. He falls to his bottom before lying down.

"How's our cat?"

Our cat? I like the idea of Pool being *our* cat.

"He's good. Settling in. I left him today to go have dinner with my parents and came home to my house being just as I left it, so that's good news. Also, I found out that Miss Ina is actually my landlord. She said I can keep him, so I don't have to worry about giving him up or finding a new place to live. I don't think I *could* give him up now that I have him."

"I would have kept him at my place if it was a problem for you. Pets are allowed in my building without much of a deposit."

"That's good to know."

"I'll have to pay that anyways since I liked having you in my space. When you stay over, you can bring him with you."

"Oh," I whisper, not sure what to say to that. I liked being at his place, too, and I like the idea of staying with him again.

"What's that 'oh' about?" he asks quietly.

"I guess I never really thought about staying over there more than once. I . . . I like the idea. It was nice going to bed with you and waking up with you."

"Good," he says, and I snuggle deeper into my covers. "Are you in bed now?"

"Yeah. I have to open the salon tomorrow, so I'm trying to get to sleep."

"Get some rest, Princess. I'll call you tomorrow evening when I have a chance."

"Be safe," I whisper.

"Always," he whispers back before hanging up. Setting my cell down on my side table, I squeeze my eyes closed.

"Pool, I really, really like him. Do you think I'm an idiot?" I ask, running my fingers over his soft fur. He starts to purr. "I need to tell him what's going on before this ends up like a really bad romance movie and my heart gets splattered all over the place," I tell him, having no idea how right I am about that.

Chapter 12

PROVING A POINT

LIBBY

When I hear the knock on the door, my stomach flutters. Even though it's only been two days since I've seen Antonio, I've missed him like crazy. Swinging the door open, I don't greet him or even give him time to open his mouth. I jump into his arms. Luckily, he's quick, so he catches me. His hands go under my ass as I wrap my legs around his hips and my arms around his shoulders. Then I drop my mouth down to his as he walks us back into my apartment, kicking the door closed once we're inside. He carries me to the couch, and we both go down, with me still attached to him.

"I missed this," I tell him as his mouth leaves mine and trails down my neck to the top of my breast.

"Me, too." I feel him smile against my skin, then see it when he pulls his face back to look at me. "That was the kind of greeting I could get used to," he says.

I start to laugh. "I kinda lost all thought about being classy and normal when I heard you knock on the door. I'm sure Miss Ina would frown on me greeting you like that if she knew I did."

"And I kinda don't give a fuck. I loved it." He smiles, running his fingers through my hair. "Have you eaten?"

"Earlier."

"Anything besides junk food?" he asks.

I look over his shoulder briefly while I shrug.

"Right." He grins, then laughs when Pool jumps up onto the couch next to my head and shoves his face where Antonio's fingers are running through my hair so that he can get some love, too.

"I think he missed you," I tell him as he sits back and picks Pool up. He holds him against his chest.

"He gained weight."

"I thought so, too, but I wasn't sure." I run my fingers along the top of Pool's head. "I know that he likes to eat. He's already perfected a cute little pout to get treats whenever he wants them."

"He's been good?"

"Yeah, really good. He's sweet." I smile at him as he climbs up Antonio's shirt to his shoulder, then stands there, looking around. "It's nice having him around to keep me company."

My cell phone rings. Picking it up off the coffee table, I answer. "Hello?"

"Is Libby Reed available?" a man asks.

"This is her." I smile at Antonio when Pool leaps off his shoulder and jumps to the back of the couch.

"We're downstairs with your delivery."

"Awesome. Come on in. The door's open—just come up the stairs," I tell him. He hangs up.

"Who's that?" Antonio asks.

An excited smile lights my face.

"My new bed." I rush to the door as two men come up the stairs with a mattress.

"New bed?" Antonio asks from the couch.

My eyes go back to him.

"With Mac now living with Wesley, I get the whole room to myself. Which means I can finally stop sleeping on the twin. Today some people came and bought the twins, and now my new bed is here," I explain excitedly.

I step back to let the guys through the open door.

"Where do you want it?" one of them asks, looking at me.

"Right through there." I point to the bedroom.

They head that way, then come out a few seconds later.

"Be back with the rest. While we're doing that, you mind filling this out?"

"No problem." I take the paper from him and fill out the highlighted information. When they come back up, they bring the box spring and the metal frame. I didn't get a headboard because I figured I could go online and order one when I know what I want. When they leave after assembling the bed, I rush to my room and jump on it, bouncing once and then laughing when Antonio comes down on top of me.

"This is much better," he says.

I smile. "I thought you'd appreciate it."

"Yeah." He touches his mouth to mine. "You want me to help you make it?"

"If you don't mind."

He stands and pulls me up with him, then orders, "Get the sheets."

Rolling my eyes, I go to the living room and grab the bags I left there earlier. I bring them to the bedroom.

Hearing him laugh, I look. "What?" I ask.

"My mom . . ." He shakes his head.

"What?" I frown, not understanding what his mom has to do with my new sheets or why he thinks it's so funny.

"Did my mom give those to you?" he questions.

My frown grows deeper.

"No."

"Really?" His frown matches the one on my face.

"Yes, really. Why?"

"My mom showed up at my place a few days ago with that *exact* bedspread and sheet set. She said she thought you'd like them. She tried to convince me to put them on my bed."

"Your mom bought sheets she'd thought *I'd* like for *your* bed?" I repeat in horror.

He ignores me and continues, "I refused to take them. No fucking way am I sleeping on flowers."

"You won't sleep on flowers?" I repeat as I look at the floral sheets and comforter, then back at him, raising a brow. "Do you think you won't be able to . . . you know"—my eyes go to his zipper—"function in floral sheets?"

"Let's get the sheets on the bed and find out," he growls, prowling toward me.

I laugh, backing up.

"I don't want to disable your manhood wit—"

I laugh harder as he grabs me around the waist, cutting off my words by dropping his mouth to mine and thrusting his tongue between my lips for a very deep, very wet kiss that is over too quickly. "Now I have a point to make, Princess." He takes the set of sheets out of my hand and opens the package. We make quick work of making my bed; then he throws me down on top of it, coming down on me once more. "You feel that?" he asks, thrusting his hips into mine.

I squirm under him when his erection grinds against my clit.

"Does that feel like I'm disabled to you?"

"No . . ." I swallow hard, thinking he definitely does not feel disabled at all.

"I get hard just thinking about you." His hand skims up my side, under my shirt, and he cups my breast over my bra. "All I can think about is getting inside of you." He kisses me again while his thumb and middle finger pull my nipple.

My back arches, and my legs wrap around his hips to pull him closer. Smiling against my mouth, he releases my nipple and leans back quickly to help me out of my top and bra.

The moment his warm lips wrap around my nipple, I moan, "Antonio."

"Right here." He moves to my other breast while my hands explore his chest and abs under his shirt. Needing to feel his skin against mine, I push his shirt up. He leans back until he pulls it off over his head.

"Yes," I whisper as his weight settles into me. "Don't stop," I plead, feeling his fingers skim down my stomach to the top of my jeans and right into my panties. The first touch of his fingers against my clit has my eyes rolling back into my head.

"Look at me, Princess," he demands. I open my eyes to focus on him. "Do you want to come?"

His thumb is still circling my clit, two fingers working me, giving me nothing and everything at the same time. "Yes," I rasp.

"Let's get you out of these jeans." He leans back and helps me get rid of them; then he's back over me with his hand between my legs. "Wet," he groans against my mouth.

I slide my hand down his chest, then unhook his jeans. When I get my hand wrapped around his cock, my pussy spasms.

"Antonio." I open my eyes to find his already on me. "Please. I'm ready."

His eyes flare, and his jaw gets tight. "Baby, I don—"

"Please," I cut him off. Releasing him, I slide my hands up his chest and hold his face between my palms. "I'm ready."

"Are you sure?" he asks, resting his forehead to mine.

God, he's so sweet and so perfect.

I love that he wants to make sure I'm ready. I love that he's not pressuring me.

"Yes, I'm sure." I lift my head and touch my mouth to his. I whisper against his lips, "Please make love to me." His eyes flare again on the word *love*; then his mouth is on mine, and he's kissing me hard. So hard that I feel branded by his lips.

When his mouth leaves mine, he takes his wallet out of his back pocket and gets out a condom. He lays it on the bed near my head, then kicks off his boots and jeans. Seeing all of him for the first time, my mouth goes dry. He really is perfect—from his handsome face to his cut collarbones, hard pecs, tight abs, the V of his waist that leads to his cock. It's hard and thick.

"Stop looking at it like that," he says. My eyes fly up to meet his. "You're going to give him performance anxiety."

"Is that a real thing?" I ask.

He laughs, grabbing hold of my ankle and tugging me down the bed.

"If it is, I don't want now to be when I find out." His hips settle between mine as his warm body comes to rest over me. "You sure about this?" he asks gently, sliding his fingers through my hair.

Looking up into his eyes, I know this is right. "This is what I've been holding out for . . . I mean, I've been waiting for *you* to . . . god." I cover my face with my hands, feeling like an idiot.

I feel his body shaking over mine.

"So damn cute." He pulls my hands from my face. "Breathe for me, Princess."

Breathe? How the hell does he expect me to breathe when he's around?

"I promise I'll take care of you," he says gently. My throat starts to get tight. "Kiss me," he urges, dipping his head closer to mine.

Arching my neck, I touch my mouth to his, then whimper when his fingers slide between my wet folds.

"Yes," I breathe into his mouth while one finger slides inside of me.

"Circle your hips in sync with my finger," he says.

I do, and then he adds another finger to the pressure, making my back bow off the bed while his thumb rolls against my oversensitive clit.

"I'm . . ." I start to feel like I'm going to come, but he pulls his hand away. My eyes fly open, and I stare up at him while he reaches for the condom, rips the package open with his teeth, then uses one hand to deftly slide it on.

"You're ready," he grunts, sliding the head of his cock over my clit and entrance before placing the tip inside and slowly sliding in.

Wrapping my legs around his hips, my fingers dig into his shoulders as he fills me slowly. There isn't any real pain, but there is pressure and a feeling of being full . . . so full.

"Oh," I breathe, looking into his eyes as he goes still, deep inside me. He's so deep that I know I will always feel him there.

"You okay?"

"Yes," I whisper.

He links our fingers together, bringing them up to rest beside my head. He settles his hips deeper into mine before pulling out and sliding back in slowly.

"You feel so good." His mouth takes mine in another brutal kiss while he keeps the slow, sensual pace of sliding in and out of me. When his mouth leaves mine again and he leans back to look at me, I swear I feel my heart fly right out of my chest and into his like it belongs to him. His eyes drop to our connection, and I watch them close before he looks at me once more. "I've never seen anything more beautiful than you taking me."

My hold on him tightens in every way, and I circle my hips. I need more—I'm just not sure what that is. His hand pulls mine down between us, and he uses both our fingers to swirl over my clit. "Oh god," I gasp, my core tightening.

He grins.

"Jesus, you're so fucking responsive to the tiniest touch." He says it like it's not a bad thing at all, but I still feel my cheeks get warm.

He circles my clit faster and faster, and a knot starts to form in my lower belly and my legs start to shake. "Let go, Princess."

He nips my earlobe, and I do. My body goes still, and I let go, falling over the edge into bliss. Eyes closed, neck arched, he lets go of my hand and starts to move more quickly inside of me. The noises coming from him and me—the pants and groans, the sound of wet skin slapping against wet skin—are enough to send me into sensory overload. When his hips stop thrusting and his body jerks, I wrap my arms around his shoulders and lift my face into his neck. I don't want him to see the tears that are threatening to spill over. I never had any expectations for my first time. But it was perfect, beyond perfect. In the realm of magical. And it being with Antonio made it that much better, that much more special. Tucking his face into my neck, he rolls us over until I'm sprawled on top of him. His fingers slide softly up and down my spine.

"You okay?" he asks gently.

I nod my head, not trusting myself to speak—not yet. So many emotions threaten to close my throat. I never thought about the connection I would feel to the person I shared my first time with.

"You sure?"

"Yeah," I say quietly.

His arms tighten around me. God, I want to stay right here forever. Right in his arms, where I feel safe and wanted, free to be me even when being me is a little awkward.

"How about a bath?" he says thoughtfully.

Those stupid tears that I feel pooling in my eyes start to spill over.

"Baby . . ." He uses my hair to pull my face away from where I have it tightly tucked against his neck. "Why are you crying?"

"I . . . then you . . . then . . . that was beautiful. And you're so sweet," I blubber.

He sits up with me still in his hold and leans back against the wall.

"I'm sorry I'm ruining this."

"You're not ruining anything, Princess." He smooths my hair away from my face and looks into my eyes. "We shared something beautiful. It's a little overwhelming. I get that."

"*You're* not crying like a dork." I wipe at my cheeks, and he smiles a soft smile at me, then kisses my lips. "Gah. I don't even know why you like me," I grumble.

His expression turns serious. "I like that you're a little bit of a dork. I like that you don't think before you say things to me. I like that you look just as beautiful without makeup as you do with it. I like that you rescue wild cats and have a deeper obsession with scary movies than I do. I like you for a lot of reasons, Princess," he says.

My body goes still while my chest starts to get tight.

Oh god. Maybe my mom was right. Maybe I do love him. No, no, it's too soon. That would be crazy. I would know. I would totally know if I was in love. Right?

"I . . ."

"You can think about what you're going to say while I start us a bath."

He carefully lifts me off him, and I whimper when he slides out. He places a soft kiss on my lips, then pulls the sheet up over me before he leaves me in bed and heads naked toward my bathroom. I listen to him flush the toilet, then hear the water in the tub turn on. I roll to my side and try to get my brain to start working properly. I know logically that sex doesn't mean love, but what we shared felt like more than just sex. He said he liked me, gave me a list of reasons why. I like him, too—a lot more than I have ever liked anyone. Not only because he's gorgeous, but because he makes me feel special and cared for. Because he's sweet and gentle.

I realize I still need to tell him about the shop.

I need to do that now. I can't let any more time pass.

When he comes back out of the bathroom, he plucks me right up out of the bed and holds me against his chest as he carries me to the tub.

"I have something to tell you," I say.

His eyes come to me as he steps into the tub.

"Tell me," he says gently.

I wonder what I should say, how I should say it.

"It's about the pizzeria," I murmur.

His body gets tight behind mine as he settles us in the warm water.

"We're not talking about the pizzeria tonight," he says firmly.

"I . . ."

"Libby, not tonight."

"Okay," I agree reluctantly as he pulls me back to rest against his chest in the tub.

"I just want to hold you. I don't want to think about anything to do with work," he says gently.

My eyes close. "Sure. I . . . We'll talk about it another time," I agree as my stomach twists uncomfortably.

"Are you sore?" he asks, changing the subject while sliding his hand down my stomach, petting softly between my legs.

I shake my head.

"You sure?"

"Yes," I whisper, feeling his lips rest against my shoulder. I know I should do the right thing. I should open my mouth and tell him the truth, once and for all. I don't. Instead, I take a bath with him, order in food, then laze on my couch with him, watching a scary movie until it's time for bed. Then I go to sleep in his arms, between floral sheets.

Chapter 13

PRACTICE MAKES PERFECT

LIBBY

"Morning, Princess." Antonio greets me with a warm smile when I walk out of my bedroom still half-asleep.

When I woke up to my alarm and he wasn't next to me, I was hit with an unexpected wave of disappointment. I thought he had taken off. Then I smelled bacon cooking, and I couldn't get out of bed fast enough. I wanted to make sure that he was really here.

"Morning," I say softly.

I scoop up Pool to give him a cuddle before I go to where Antonio's standing—shirtless—in front of the stove. I tuck myself against his front, feeling his lips touch the top of my head as his arms give me a squeeze.

"Did you sleep okay?" he asks.

I tip my head back to look up at his handsome face and strong jaw, now covered in a thick layer of stubble.

I slept better than I have in two days. I don't say that. Instead, I answer softly, "Yes."

"You sore?" he asks gently.

I feel my cheeks get warm. "Not too bad."

"I'll get you some ibuprofen after you eat something." His fingers slide up my throat, and his thumb and forefinger capture my chin and pull my head back so that he can touch his mouth to mine.

The kiss is soft and sweet, but it still leaves me feeling off-balance. When his mouth leaves mine, I have to once again force my eyes open.

"So . . ." I clear my throat. "What's on your schedule today?" I let him go and step around him to get a cup of coffee.

"I need to go home to take care of some stuff, then I'm working tonight with you. I figured I'd pack a bag while I'm home. We can stay here after we close the shop—if that works for you."

"It works for me," I agree immediately.

He smiles.

I pour some creamer into my coffee, then add some sugar before hopping up onto the counter and taking a sip from my coffee cup.

"Where did you get bacon and eggs?" I ask him when he goes to the fridge and pulls out a carton of eggs that wasn't there last night.

"I ran to the corner store when I got up," he says, cracking two eggs into a pan. "You really do need to start eating more than takeout, Princess."

"Takeout is easy when I'm working all the time. I don't have to lug bags up here or cook. All I have to do is pick up my phone and dial a number to get whatever I want."

"Yeah, but when your man wants to make you breakfast and all he has to work with is old pizza and Chinese food, it makes it kind of hard."

My man? Holy cow, he's mine . . . I mean, yes, I kind of knew that already. But hearing him call himself my man makes it real.

"What?" he asks, studying me.

"I . . . I guess it just really hit me that we're together," I admit.

His face softens.

"It's weird after"—I pause to pull in a breath—"it's weird after everything that has happened between us."

Coming to where I'm standing, he forces my knees apart and wedges himself between my thighs. He takes hold of my face, gently, between his large palms.

"This is going to work," he states, looking into my eyes. "I know with the way I treated you in the past I don't deserve anything from you, but I need you to know that I'm all in. This is what I want. *You* are what I want. If I wasn't sure about us, I would not have made love to you yesterday."

"Okay," I agree quietly. My chest starts to get warm, and my heart starts to fill with hope—and something else . . . something that's a little scary to think about since this is so new.

"This is going to work," he repeats, kissing me hard.

"This is going to work," I agree when he pulls his mouth from mine.

He smiles before letting me go and turning back to the stove.

Watching him make us breakfast, all I can think is that I really hope he's right. I really hope this works.

~

With tongue and teeth licking and nipping at Antonio's neck, I pant for breath. I feel his hands roam over my backside and his cock thrust up into me. It's been two weeks since we introduced sex into our relationship, and in that time, I've become a nympho.

"Fuck, but you feel good," he groans as he uses his hold on my ass to lift me up and bring me down onto his length. "I want your mouth, Libby."

I pull my mouth from his neck and look down at him, teasing his bottom lip with my tongue and watching up close as his eyes heat up and narrow.

"Give me your mouth." He thrusts up hard, making me gasp, and I bite his bottom lip.

"Antonio," I whimper in distress when he goes still inside me, holding the tip of his cock at my entrance. "Please don't stop."

"Give me what I want," he orders. My pussy tightens. "Now, Libby," he warns.

I slide my tongue into his mouth to toy with his. Pulling my back away from the wall, he carries me across the room and settles me on the top of the table in his kitchen, his mouth never leaving mine. I dig the heels of my feet into his back and slide my fingers down his spine to his ass, pulling him against me to tell him silently what I need.

When he pulls back and smirks at me, my pussy spasms again. "You want my cock?"

Ignoring the arrogant tone in his voice, I lift my head off the table and whisper, "Please."

He doesn't make me ask again. He slides out and then back in, hard. So hard that the table shakes.

"So tight. Christ . . ." He thrusts his tongue back into my mouth while his hand slides around my hip and his thumb rolls over my clit. "Your pussy is already trying to milk me," he says, leaning back to look at where we're connected. "I love watching you take me. I love feeling your pussy clutch me like it's afraid my cock's going to disappear."

His eyes meet mine as the muscles in my lower belly start to get tight. Stars start to dance in my vision. "Oh god."

"I feel it. Let go, Princess. I got you," he says gruffly.

I give myself over to the feeling. The heels of my feet dig into his back, and my hold on him tightens as I come apart in his arms. His pace picks up as I come, and I listen to the sound of his orgasm when he follows me over the edge. He drops his forehead to my chest.

Breathing heavy, I wrap my arms around him and keep my legs tight around his hips. I'm not ready to lose our connection in any way.

"I like when you look all sweaty," I whisper when my breath has stopped coming in short, choppy pants.

"I kinda got that. You jumped me as soon as I walked in the door." He leans back to look at me, and I give him a pleased smile.

"I bet you gave at least ten women an impromptu orgasm when you were out on your run," I say, running my fingers along the underside of his strong jaw.

"I only care about *your* orgasms." He pushes my hair away from my face and studies me for a long moment before dropping his gaze to the top I have on. "I see you found another shirt. Are you keeping it, like all the others you've stolen?"

"It's not stealing if you know I have them. And yes. I think this is my new favorite. It's soft."

"I like you wearing my shirt and nothing else around my place. And I *really* like the way you greeted me wearing nothing but my shirt. But can I ask how the hell you got so wet before I even touched you?"

"I got a glimpse of you out the window before you came in from your run. I was already turned on by the time you got upstairs," I admit with a shrug and a laugh. "You've turned me into this," I say.

I lose sight of his face when he drops his mouth down to mine for a deep kiss.

"You won't be hearing me complain about that." He lifts me off the table. "I need a shower."

"Me, too. I'm all wet."

Hearing him groan, I laugh as he carries me into the bathroom and sets me down so he can turn on the water. Pulling his T-shirt over my head, I don't drop it in his clothes hamper. I take it to my overnight bag and shove it inside. I think I've taken one of his shirts each time I've stayed over at his place. I'm starting to get quite the collection.

"If you keep taking my shirts, I won't have any to wear," he tells me, tugging my hand and pulling me into the shower with him.

"You have a million shirts. It will take me forever to collect them all." I smile as his hands start to roam over my skin with a bar of soap that smells like him. "Besides, when you're working and I don't get to sleep with you, I like having them to wear to bed at night," I say.

He smiles softly before touching his lips to mine.

"You get me for two more nights."

"I know."

Last night was the first one he had off in about four days. I missed sleeping next to him, feeling him curled around me all night. Really, I just missed him. I've gotten more than a little used to having him around, waking up and having breakfast with him, working with him at the pizzeria in the evenings, then going home to his place or mine. It's been nice—more than nice. It's crazy how quickly we've fallen into a pattern of spending all our time together. He was right weeks ago: this thing between us is working out perfectly.

Well, I kind of still need to tell him about buying the shop. Every time I've attempted to bring it up, he shuts me down. So I just stopped bringing it up.

"Are you ready to have dinner with my parents tomorrow?" I ask him as I take the soap from his grasp and start to run it over the ridges and valleys of his abs.

"Yeah. I should ask you if *you're* ready."

"It will probably be horribly embarrassing, but I'm excited for you to meet Levi and Wesley. I think you guys will get along." I look up at him and add, "My mom will probably hint at marriage and babies and all kinds of other things that are way too soon to talk about right now, so don't freak out when that happens and run for the hills."

"I won't run. I'd like to remind you about my mother—it's not like she hasn't mentioned grandkids a few dozen times since we got together."

"True." Martina has clearly decided that since Antonio and I are together, we need to start popping out grandchildren—the sooner the better. "Our families are insane," I mutter, dropping my eyes back to my hands as they roam over his smooth skin.

"They are," he agrees as his fingers skim over my nipples. "That doesn't mean we can't do both our parents a favor and start practicing at making those grandkids for them," he says.

My belly dips.

"Practice does make perfect," I whisper against his lips when his mouth touches mine, and he smiles while he kisses me.

We spend the rest of the morning and afternoon practicing. By the time we're done and we have to get to work at the pizzeria, I'm pretty sure we're both pros.

Chapter 14

Dinner

Antonio

Leaning back in my chair, I smile. Dinner with Libby's family has gone off without a hitch. Fawn's husband, Levi, and Mac's boyfriend, Wesley, are both men I can see myself becoming friends with. They seem laid-back and cool. Libby's dad also seems like a good man, and I can tell that he loves his daughters and his wife.

"I really thought Aiden was going to cut off your balls when he found out that you snuck off to Vegas to marry his daughter," Wesley says to Levi with a smirk.

Levi narrows his eyes at his partner and friend. "Really? Knocking up his daughter *without* marrying her was better?" he questions with a smirk of his own.

"I didn't want to marry him," Mac says.

Wesley transfers his narrowed eyes to his pregnant girlfriend.

Chuckling, I lean back in my seat and slide my arm behind Libby, resting it on the back of her chair.

"So why did you hate Libby?"

At Fawn's question, everyone around the dinner table seems to go still. All eyes focus on me. I shift uncomfortably, then look down the table at her, wondering what to say. I shift my gaze to Aiden and squirm.

Judging by the look in his eyes, I'm thinking he's about to change his mind about liking me.

"I didn't hate her," I say, giving Libby's knee a squeeze.

"Really?" she says, crossing her hands over her chest. "You didn't hate me?"

She rolls her eyes, and I want to lean over and kiss the shit out of her to show her that I really *didn't* hate her.

"You had a really weird way of showing it," Libby says. I look at her and notice that she's frowning. "You were always so short with me, always a jerk to me whenever we were around each other."

Studying her expression, I let out a heavy breath. "My ex did a number on me, and I took it out on you," I admit.

Her frown deepens.

"So you were mean to her because of your *ex*?" Miss Ina says. I look across the table at the older woman. "Are you crazy?" Fighting back a smile, I shake my head. "You must be if you let your past decide your future."

"My ex was materialistic. Nothing I ever did for her seemed like enough. She only cared about money and designer labels. When I first met Libby, I overheard her talking about a handbag and—"

"You assumed that Libby was just like her." Miss Ina cuts me off, her eyes turning squinty, her lip curling up in disgust.

"I think that he was scared because he knew in some way that if he gave Libby a chance that he would fall in love with her," Fawn says.

My heart thumps hard because her words ring true. I've really fallen for Libby over these last few weeks, and I know I'm falling in love with her.

"Guys are always running away from love."

"Not me," Levi says.

She looks up at him and smiles wistfully. "No, not you. You ran right into love with me while I was the one trying to run away."

"I still caught you," he says. I watch him toy with the rings on her finger.

"How exactly were you a jerk to my girl?" Aiden asks, his voice a deep rumble.

My body goes tight.

Shit.

"I—"

"I can't believe you were a jerk to me just because you overheard me talking about a bag I wanted to buy," Libby says, sounding pissed. I move my gaze to her. "Seriously? That was your reasoning for treating me like crap? I work hard for everything I have. I have always worked hard for the things I want." She shakes her head.

She looks like she's going to toss her napkin on the table and sock me one.

"I told you I made a lot of assumptions about you."

"Yeah." She shakes her head, pulling her eyes from mine. "Obviously it showed I was *so* materialistic right? I mean, I was just dripping in designer clothes, right? I would have you know I have never paid full price for anything that I own. I always look for a bargain."

"I still would like to know how you treated her," Aiden says.

From my side, Wesley urges under his breath, "Abort! Abort!" I hear Mac start to giggle.

"Who wants dessert?" Katie asks suddenly, pushing back from the table. "I made a cake."

"I'll help you." Libby starts to stand, but I tighten my hold on her thigh before she can get up.

"I'm sorry for how I treated you. I shouldn't have assumed that you were like her. I should have taken the chance and gotten to know you."

"Yeah, you should have," she agrees, trying to get up once more.

"Don't be pissed."

"Family dinners are always so much fun," Mac jokes.

Libby looks over my shoulder at her sister and glares.

"Princess," I call, and Libby's eyes meet mine. "I'm sorry," I tell her. Her jaw ticks. "I was an asshole. The way I treated you had nothing to do with you and everything to do with me and where my head was at." She lets out a huff, relaxes into her chair. "I'm sorry." I lean over to kiss the side of her head. I hear her sigh.

"You're lucky you've proven that you can be sweet," she tells me, looking into my eyes. "Otherwise I would leave the table and let my dad have a few words with you."

"You wouldn't."

"I so would."

"Your dad's scary," I say just loud enough for her to hear.

She smiles. "He also owns more than one gun. You should probably remember that." She pats my cheek. "Big ones *and* small ones."

I swallow the lump in my throat and look over at her father. *Would he really shoot me?* I remember the glare he aimed at me. He would shoot me without thinking twice.

"What are you two talking about? Speak up so that the rest of us can hear you," Miss Ina says. I start to laugh and watch Libby do the same.

"Nothing, Miss Ina," Libby says right before she leans forward to kiss me and let me know that we're okay.

～

"I have something I want to tell you," Libby says.

I'm walking out of the bathroom, where I just got rid of the condom we used. I glance at the clock to see how much time we have before she needs to get ready for work and I need to take off for my run.

"What's that?" I get back into bed, then drag her across the mattress to me and pull the blankets up and over us.

"It's about the pizzeria," she starts.

I feel every muscle in my body get tense, and my arms tighten around her. She's brought up the pizzeria more than a few times over the last couple of weeks. And no matter how many times I've explained my feelings about the shop, I haven't been able to deter her from mentioning it time and time again. I know she loves the place, and I know she hates the idea of someone else owning it. She probably wants to talk to me about reconsidering taking over from my parents.

"Libby . . ."

"Please hear me out," she urges, turning toward me and resting her hands against my bare chest.

"I don't want anything to do with the pizzeria," I cut her off. "I also don't want to talk about it," I grit out through clenched teeth.

"But—"

"But nothing, Princess," I say, trying not to let my voice go up a register. I decide I finally need to make her try and understand. "You didn't grow up with your parents working there seven days a week, twelve hours a day, Libby. You didn't spend most of your weekends answering phones and taking orders. You didn't have to fall asleep in the back room in a sleeping bag because the restaurant closed late on Friday and you had no choice but to stay with your parents. You didn't miss out on time with your parents because they had a business to run. Your dad didn't miss your games because he couldn't find anyone to cover the shop for him. You haven't watched that place slowly kill your father over the years."

"I—"

"No." I cut her off again. I toss back the blankets and get out of bed. "We're not talking about it." I walk toward the chair where my clothes are.

"Where are you going?" she asks, getting up on her knees, her eyes going wide with alarm.

"Gonna head out for a run," I say, pulling on my sweats and a sweatshirt.

"But—"

"You need to get ready for work. You have to catch a cab soon."

"We *need* to talk about the shop." She grabs my hand, and I shake my head to deny her wish.

"We *don't* need to talk about the shop. It's not my problem anymore. It's done, Libby. Someone else is buying it. Leave it be for once."

"I—" she starts.

I cut her off with a swift kiss.

"I'll see you in a couple days. I'll call you tonight when I get a chance." I turn and leave the room, ignoring her when she calls out to me again. Grabbing my key and cell phone off the counter in the kitchen, I shove both in my pocket before putting on my sneakers and leaving my apartment. Once I'm out of the building, I run until it feels like my legs are about to give out on me before heading home. When I let myself back into my apartment, Libby's gone. I knew she would be, which is good. I didn't want her to leave like that, leave with me upset, leave while she was probably upset also. I know that she feels different about the pizzeria than I do, but she didn't grow up like I did. She just needs to let it go. Hopefully once the new owner takes over, we won't have to talk about it ever again.

Chapter 15

I Must Be Dying

LIBBY

"I'm looking for Libby."

The male voice sounds familiar. I frown, trying to figure out where I know that voice from and why there is a man here looking for me at all.

"And you are?" Peggy asks.

I quickly wash my hands and rinse them off, then grab a paper towel and start to dry them.

"Walter," the voice answers as I push through the swinging door. I come to a dead stop when a familiar set of blue eyes rests on me.

"Walter," I whisper in shock at seeing him again. Especially here, of all places.

"Hey." He smiles, shoving his hands in the front pockets of his trousers, looking a little uncomfortable. "I know I should have called, but when I spoke with Palo this morning, he told me you were buying a pizzeria. I wanted to come check it out, and to tell you congratulations."

"Buying a pizzeria?"

My heart sinks and my stomach coils. I turn to look at Antonio, whose voice is filled with tension. It's been three days since I left his apartment in tears after trying to tell him that I was the buyer. We've talked since then, but the conversations have always been short.

"I . . ."

"*You're* the one buying the shop?" he asks, his jaw clenching and unclenching while he waits for my answer.

"Yes," I whisper.

"What the fuck?" he barks, making me jump.

"I was going to tell you," I say quickly while I take a step toward him. He takes a step back, holding up his hand between us.

"I *tried* to tell you," I say softly, holding my hands together. Tears start to sting my eyes. "You always shut me down."

"It's been *weeks* since my parents told me they got an offer on the shop. Weeks, Libby. In that time, I've spent almost every day with you."

"I know. I tried to tell you," I repeat softly as my chest starts to get tight. "I'm sorry . . . I tried."

"Sorry? What are you sorry for, exactly?"

"I'm sorry I didn't tell you sooner. I should have told you sooner."

"You didn't fucking tell me *at all*," he growls, his eyes shooting behind me to where I know Walter is standing.

"I know. I was going to—" I cut off my own words when his eyes harden. "Can we talk about this in private?" I ask, feeling everyone's eyes on us.

"I think your time for talking is up."

"Antonio . . ." I try to stop him, but he storms past me.

I follow after him. When he goes inside the office, I shut the door behind me. "Just please hear me out," I beg as I watch him put on his coat and hat.

"Why should I listen to you now?" He turns on me, and the anger I see in his gaze makes my breath freeze in my lungs.

"I'm sorry. I knew I should have told you sooner. I knew I should have, but at first I didn't think you'd understand why I wanted this place. I thought you'd try to talk me out of buying it. Then you wouldn't listen to me whenever I tried to bring it up."

"I guess now you'll *never* know what I would have said or done."

He moves for the door, but I step in front of it.

"Get out of my way, Libby."

"Antonio, please. Just . . . let's just calm down and talk about this."

"It's too late. We have not one fucking thing to talk about. Not anymore," he growls.

My heart doesn't just sink; it shatters in my chest, cutting me wide open.

"Good luck, Libby. And good fucking riddance."

He opens the door and then leaves, slamming it closed. I start to breathe heavily, and tears blur my vision. I know I can't let him leave without talking to me. I open the door and run out after him.

"*Chiquita*, give him time to cool down." Hector stops me at the front door of the shop, and I finally let the sob out. I turn toward him and bury my face against his wide chest.

"Give her here, babe. Get her coat for me. I'll take her home," Peggy says, taking me from Hector and wrapping her arms around me. "Calm down, Libby. It will be okay."

"I messed up," I whimper. Her arms tighten. "I ruined it."

"It will be okay," she repeats gently. She lets me go and holds out my coat so I can put it on. "Come on. Let's get you home. You'll see. Everything will be okay."

"It won't be okay," I deny, looking at her.

Her eyes fill with sympathy. "It will. Just give him time," she says gently. I shake my head. "I'll walk you home."

"No, I'm okay. I'll be okay." Worry fills her features as I wipe away the wet from my cheeks. "Really, I'm okay." I pull in a deep breath, willing myself to stop crying.

"Libby, I'm sorry. I didn't know," Walter says.

My eyes go to where he's standing—still with his hands tucked into the front pockets of his trousers.

"It's okay. It was going to come out one way or another."

"I—"

"It's okay," I repeat, cutting him off.

I turn for the door and run out. I head straight home. As soon as I make it inside the entryway, a sob rips from my chest. I stop, lift my hair away from my face, and try to breathe.

"Libby?" Spinning around, I find Miss Ina standing in her open apartment door. "What on earth happened, child?" she whispers with wide, worry-filled eyes.

I cover my face with both my hands and cry harder.

"Come on." She grabs my arm and leads me slowly into her apartment, where she forces me to sit on her couch before taking a seat next to me. "Now tell me what happened," she urges, wrapping her arm awkwardly around my shoulder.

"Antonio found out that I'm buying the shop."

"Was he mad that you're buying it?" she asks, sounding slightly confused.

I shake my head.

"No . . . he"—my head jerks from side to side—"he was mad that I didn't tell him about it . . . that I didn't tell him that I was going to buy it."

"Oh dear."

"Yeah." I try to suck in a lungful of air, but it's difficult with how tight my chest feels. "He said, 'Good luck and good riddance.' Good riddance . . . god . . . we're done, and it's all my fault for not telling him something that I should have told him weeks ago. Before things between us got serious."

"Give him time to calm down. He'll come to his senses. It was just a shock, that's all."

"He won't. I know he won't."

"He'll come around, child. It will all be okay."

"He didn't even want to hear me out when I tried to talk to him."

"Men are stubborn like that, Libby. It's best you learn that now. He'll come around, and when he does, you two will work this out."

"Why does my chest hurt so badly?" I whisper, looking into Miss Ina's dark eyes.

Her face softens. She doesn't answer my question; she just wraps her arms around me and gives me a hug.

"Am I dying?" I ask, hugging her back.

"What?" She pulls back to look at me.

"You're hugging me and my chest is hurting. I must be dying of a heart attack."

"You're not dying, child. It's called heart*break*."

"Great." More tears fall down my cheeks. "Heartbreak sucks. Remind me to never fall in love again," I say, then feel my eyes widen. "No." I shake my head when her eyes turn knowing. "I'm not in love with him. I'm not. I can't be. It's too soon."

"Hush." She covers my mouth with her hand. "Love doesn't always happen when we expect it to. It doesn't always happen with fireworks and explosions. Sometimes it sneaks up on you silently, when you least expect it."

"I'm not." I try again, my voice muffled by her hand.

She shakes her head.

"You are, and it's going to be okay," she says gently.

I want to believe her, I really do. But I saw the look in his eyes before he left. It wasn't just me not telling him about buying the pizzeria—it was something deeper than that.

"It will be okay. One way or another, it will be okay, Libby. That I can promise you."

Grabbing her hand, I pull it away from my mouth. "What if he doesn't forgive me?"

"Then he doesn't deserve you, and you will find someone who does. Someone who will cherish you exactly like you deserve."

"What if—"

"Enough with the what-ifs, child." She lets me go and stands. "Right now I'm going to make you some tea. Then you're going to go upstairs, wash that makeup that's running down your face away, and go to bed. Tomorrow you're going to start a new day knowing that, one way or another, things will work out."

"Okay," I agree, watching her walk slowly to the kitchen.

When she comes back, she hands me a cup of tea that smells like peppermint. I drink it while she watches in silence. My mind is in turmoil.

~

"Is she sleeping?" I swear I hear my sister Fawn, but I know I must be dreaming.

"Her eyes are closed, so my guess is yes," Mac answers.

I frown. Why am I dreaming about my sisters?

"Should we wake her up?" At that question, I blink my eyes open and stare at my sisters, who are both standing over my bed. "Never mind. She's awake now," Fawn says, and her face softens. "Hey."

"What are you guys doing here?" I ask, looking between my sisters. They both have concerned looks on their faces.

"Mom called us," Mac answers, taking a seat on the bed. She jumps up a second later when she accidentally sits on Pool, who was under the blankets.

"You got a cat." Fawn picks up the kitten and holds him against her chest.

"That's Pool," I tell her, feeling my chest get tight.

Why did I let Antonio name him? Now I'm going to be reminded of him every time I say the name.

"He's cute," Mac says, taking him from Fawn.

"Why did Mom call you?" I ask, bringing the situation back into focus. They both look at me.

"Miss Ina called her last night and told her what happened."

"Great." I close my eyes, wishing that I could go back to sleep and wake up with last night being nothing but a really bad dream.

"How are you doing?" Fawn asks, sliding my hair away from my face.

My heart feels like it's been ripped out of my body and stomped all over, then run over a few times. I open my eyes and sit up.

"I'm okay. You guys didn't need to come over."

"We're your sisters. Of course we needed to come over." Mac sighs as Fawn walks around to take a seat next to me on the bed. "We know we've sucked lately. We're sorry for not being here for you."

"You both have your lives to live. I get it. It's okay," I say quietly as my throat starts to get tight.

"It's not okay that we've gotten so caught up in what's going on in our own lives that we've neglected our baby sister," Mac says, picking up my hand and giving it a squeeze. "What happened?" she asks.

I drop my head forward and look at her hand holding mine. Then I tell them everything that's happened between Antonio and me—including the fact that I gave him my virginity.

"I really am a jerk," Fawn says when I finish. "I had no idea you were going through so much."

"I didn't tell anyone." I shrug, and she leans into my side while I keep my eyes on my lap.

"I know. But I also didn't ask. I'm sorry," she says quietly.

"It's okay."

"It's not okay," Mac says.

I lift my eyes to her when I hear the angry tone in her voice.

"I knew something was going on with you and Antonio, and I didn't ask you about it. I should have asked you about it."

"I don't know that I would have told you anything—even if you did ask," I admit. Her face softens. "Now I don't think it matters anyway, since I doubt I will ever see him again."

Hearing Fawn snort, I look over at her. "Once he cools off, he'll come around."

"He was really mad."

"Yeah, and he has a reason to be mad. But he will realize that he overreacted and come around. Just give him some time."

I don't think that she's right. He was good at pretending to hate me for years—and that was before I ever gave him a real reason to dislike me. Now that he has ammunition and a reason for why he shouldn't trust me, I have a feeling that he's going to use that to stay away from me for good. I don't know exactly what his ex did, but I'm sure that, in one way or another, she lied to him and kept things from him. He's probably put me right into the same box he put her into.

"I think you need alcohol," Mac says.

I look over at the alarm on my bedside table. "It's nine in the morning."

"It's five o'clock somewhere," Fawn sings, and I laugh. "Come on. Get dressed. I'm going to search and see what I can find in your kitchen." She shoves me out of bed, then scoots out behind me.

I grab a pair of sweats and one of my old shirts, then go into the bathroom and shut the door behind me. When I look in the mirror, I groan. I didn't do as Miss Ina suggested and wash my face when I got home last night. Instead, I got into bed and held Pool while I cried some more. Grabbing a face wipe, I clean my old makeup off my face, then tie my hair up into a ponytail before I get dressed. I head into the living room and find Fawn in the kitchen, cooking. Mac is opening the bottle of white zinfandel that was in my fridge. Looking down when Pool circles my feet, I smile, pick him up, and kiss the top of his head.

"Here." Mac hands me a glass full to the top with wine. I take it from her and raise a brow. "Drink up, sister."

"I should probably call Martina before I get too drunk and explain to her what happened," I say before taking a large drink of cold wine.

"Do you think she's going to upset you more if you talk to her?" Fawn asks, looking troubled.

I shake my head.

"She knew I didn't want to tell Antonio about purchasing the shop. I asked her and Tony not to tell him. I don't want him to get to them before I have a chance to tell them that he knows and that he's pissed, though."

"I still don't really understand why you didn't want to tell him," Mac says, studying me.

"That's because my reasons were totally stupid—in hindsight." I set down my glass of wine and grab my cell phone from my purse. When I turn on the screen, I see that I have a few missed calls from my mom and sisters. Ignoring my mom's calls for now, I dial Martina's number. I put my phone to my ear as I take a seat on the couch, keeping hold of Pool.

"I knew this would happen," Martina says when she answers. My eyes slide closed. "Are you okay?"

"No," I whisper.

"Oh, *cara*. I'm so sorry."

"It's okay."

"It's not, but it will be," she says as I bury my face against Pool's soft fur.

"Have you seen him? Is he okay?"

"He stopped by this morning to talk to me and his father. He wasn't in the mood to listen to anything we had to say, so he left."

"I'm sorry I dragged you and Tony into this stupid mess." I sigh.

"It's fine. I still don't understand why you didn't want to tell him, but Tony says that he does. Maybe I will try to have him explain it to me."

"Maybe he can explain it to me, too," I mutter.

She laughs. "Are you going to be okay, *cara*? Do you want me to come over?"

"My sisters are here with me, but thank you. I'm glad you're not mad at me."

"Of course I'm not mad at you. Us women need to stick together. My son will come around—just give him time."

Give him time . . . I swear if I hear that one more time, I might lose my mind.

"I'll give him time," I agree, thinking that he's got all the time in the world. I did wrong. I messed up by keeping something from him. But shouldn't he have at least taken the time to listen to me when I tried to explain things to him? He should have known after all the times I tried to talk to him about the shop that I had a good reason for doing so.

"We'll talk soon, *cara*."

"Soon."

I hang up, then dial my mom's number.

"Honey," Mom whispers. I squeeze my eyes closed. "Are you okay?"

"Fawn and Mac are here," I answer without answering.

"Good. I'm coming into the city. I'm getting ready to leave now."

"Mom, you don't need to do that."

"Yes, I do," she affirms. "I love you. I'll be there soon. We will talk then."

Great.

"Okay," I agree. "Love you, too." I hang up, then look over at Fawn and Mac. "Mom's on her way."

"You're going to need more alcohol," Mac mutters, picking up my still-full wineglass and bringing it over to me.

Hearing pounding on the door, my heart leaps in my chest. It crashes when Miss Ina shouts, "Open the door!"

"Great. This is just getting better by the second."

"At least you know you're loved," Fawn tells me, handing me a plate of pancakes.

Mac opens the door to let Miss Ina inside.

"Took you long enough," Miss Ina snaps at Mac.

"It took me half a second to open the door," Mac replies with a roll of her eyes.

"Whatever," Miss Ina grumbles. Then her eyes move over to me.

"Are you okay?"

"Peachy." I hold up my glass of wine.

"Morning drinking. Lord. It's worse than I thought."

"Are you going to hug me again to make it better?" I ask her, and her dark eyes narrow. "Just asking."

"Your mom is on her way. When she gets here, we're all going to Bloomingdale's."

"What?"

"Therapy, child. *I'll* even buy you something."

I really must be broken, because for the first time in my life, shopping is not something I want to do.

"I'd rather stay in."

"And what? Get drunk and watch TV?" She shakes her head. "We're getting you out of this apartment for the day, getting your mind off things." She pulls her eyes from me before I can tell her that I'd really rather not. She looks at Fawn. "Where's *my* coffee?"

"I didn't know you wanted coffee." Fawn flashes an amused smile at the old woman.

"You didn't ask. What's with you kids nowadays and your lack of manners?"

"Miss Ina, stop being a grouch," I tell her before taking a huge gulp of wine. "And I'm not going anywhere. I'm staying in, drinking wine, watching movies, then going to bed early since I have to work at the salon tomorrow."

"Fine," she huffs as Fawn brings her a cup of coffee.

I smile at both my sisters, then settle back against the couch with my pancakes.

An hour later, Mom shows up. When I tell her that I don't feel up to going out, she leaves to get us all lunch. We eat in front of the TV—even Miss Ina eats her sandwich sitting on the couch next to me. Okay, so she complains the whole time about eating in front of the TV, but I ignore that and focus on the good part. The being-surrounded-by-love part. I also drink wine. Lots of it from my never-empty wineglass. We watch movies—all of them scary—and when everyone leaves, I go to bed and once again cry myself to sleep while holding on to Pool. He doesn't seem to care at all that his fur is soaked through.

Chapter 16

SWALLOW MY PRIDE

ANTONIO

When my cab drives past the pizzeria, I can't help myself. I look out the window and see the new sign over the shop: **PRINCESS PIZZA**. She changed the name to Princess Pizza, with a bright-pink fucking sign.

Fuck . . .

My chest tightens, and nausea rolls in my stomach. Seeing the new name on the shop doesn't hurt—it kills. It's been two weeks, *two fucking weeks*, since I've seen Libby. In that time, I've gone from being pissed at her to pissed at myself. I fucked up. I let my anger get the best of me, and I walked away when I should have stuck around. I should have let her explain. Hell, I should have let her explain all the times she tried to talk to me about the pizzeria before I found out she was buying it. I never did. Every single time she started to bring up the shop, I would shut her down. I didn't want to hear her tell me that she thought I should take it over from my parents, that she thought I was making a mistake. I had put her right into the same box with my ex and closed the fucking lid on them both again.

I rub my palm against my chest to try and get rid of the pain there, even though I know it's useless. Somehow I ended up falling in love with Libby. I don't know how it happened or when it happened, but there is no denying that I love her. I love her. And now . . . now I don't know how to get back to where we were before I so royally fucked things up between us. Honestly, I'm scared as hell that she won't want me back when I finally get up the courage to go to her.

"You're here," my cab driver says when he pulls up in front of my parents' place.

I haven't only been avoiding Libby these last two weeks—I've also been avoiding my parents. I always felt like the pizzeria was the one thing in life that my parents and I disagreed about. My dad and mom have always loved the shop, and I have always resented it for taking them away from me when I was growing up. Over the years, I have become so focused on the bad that I forgot about the good times I had at the pizzeria as a kid. I forgot about my dad teaching me to make pizzas, forgot about my mom throwing me birthday parties at the shop, forgot about any sports team I was on eating for free after each game. I also knew my father was disappointed in me for not following in his footsteps. That guilt I've been carrying around only seemed to get heavier when he had his heart attack. He said he understood my reasons for turning down his offer, but I could still see the defeat in his eyes when he told me he and Mom were going to sell the shop.

Making it up the brick steps, I ring the bell. I wait with my hands tucked in the front pockets of my jeans. My mom peeks through the side window, and a relieved smile lights up her face.

"You know you don't have to knock or ring the bell. I gave you a key for a reason," she says as soon as she opens the door.

"I left my key at home," I explain as I bend down to kiss her cheek. "Is Dad around?"

"Yes. He's here. He's in the living room, yelling at the television."

"Who's playing?"

"A red team and a blue team; that's about all I know," she says with a laugh as I follow her to the living room.

My dad is indeed yelling at a soccer game on the TV. As soon as I step into the room, though, he reaches for the remote and shuts it off.

"Took you long enough to get here," he says by way of greeting.

The tension I've been holding on to releases instantly.

"Sorry. I should have come sooner."

"You should have," he agrees. He gets up from his recliner and walks toward me. Meeting him halfway across the room, I wrap my arms around him.

"I'm sorry."

"It's not me that you need to apologize to," he says gruffly, pounding his fist into my back.

"I know," I agree when he lets me go.

"She's a good girl. I hope you figure out a way to forgive her for not telling you, but I want you to know now that I get why she didn't. You're not the easiest person to talk to when it comes to discussing the pizzeria."

"She tried to tell me. I just didn't want to listen," I admit.

He shakes his head, takes a seat back in his recliner. I take a seat across from him, on the couch.

"What are you going to do to win her back?"

"I don't fucking know." I scrub my hands down my face. "I fucked up, big-time. I've been hiding like a coward since then."

"My son's not a coward," he states firmly. I meet his gaze. "You need to go to her."

"What if she says she doesn't want to see me again? Worse, what if she tells me to fuck off?"

"I can't imagine Libby saying that," Mom offers as she comes into the room and sits next to me.

"Have you seen her?" I ask, looking at her.

"I saw her this morning. I went to the shop to help her with a few things in the office that she didn't know how to do," she says. She reaches over, taking my hand in hers. "She's doing as well as can be expected."

"I miss her," I say, fighting the urge to rub the palm of my hand against my chest right over my heart. "I love her."

"I know you do," Mom says sympathetically, giving my hand a squeeze. "She renamed the shop Princess Pizza. I think that tells you something about the way she feels for you, too."

"I saw the new sign," I admit. "It's really pink." I laugh, and it sounds rough and foreign.

"This is Libby we're talking about. She's all about being a girl. I think it's going to be a hit. She's bringing something new to the neighborhood and the business. Your father and I have been really impressed by her plans."

I'm not surprised. She's got a good head on her shoulders, and she's a hard worker. I know that with her running the shop, it's going to be successful.

"Go to her. Talk to her," Dad says. I look at him. "She's probably at the shop right now. She's been there every day, getting things ready for the grand reopening."

"When's that?"

"In two days," Mom says. "She's having a big party to celebrate. Your dad and I will be going to show our support. Maybe you can come."

"Maybe it's best I talk to her before then. I don't want to ambush her at her party and ruin it for her."

"Either way, I'm sure she'd like to see you," she says solemnly.

I let out a deep breath.

"Are we okay?" I ask, looking between my parents. My dad frowns while Mom's brows pull together. "I know you were both disappointed in me for not wanting to take over the shop. I hate that I let you both down."

"You haven't let us down. We're proud of you, proud of the kind of man you are. All we want is to see you happy, Antonio. We would never try to force our own dreams down your throat."

"I am happy—or I was." I *was* happy until I ruined things with Libby, until I proved to her once again what an asshole I can be.

"You'll get Libby back and find happiness again, son," Dad says quietly.

Fuck, but I hope he's right.

If he's not, I don't know what I will do. I thought that I loved my ex, but it didn't feel like this. I'm in love with Libby. I know that if I can't find a way to get her back, I will never find the kind of happiness and love that she gave me again.

"I'll go talk to her."

I get up and hug both my parents before heading out the door and catching a cab.

When my driver parks across the street from the pizzeria, I start to pay my fare, but then I see Libby walk out of the shop wearing a pair of tight blue jeans and a simple long-sleeve T-shirt. Her hair is tied up in a bun, and her face is clean of makeup. She looks over her shoulder at a man walking out of the pizzeria behind her and smiles at him.

Walter . . . ? What the fuck is he doing with her, and why the fuck is she smiling at him?

I fight the urge to get out of the cab and bash his face in.

I absently rub my chest over my heart as they head down the block.

She's moved on. She's already moved on. I let things go too long, and she started seeing someone else. How the fuck did I lose her already?

"You gonna get out, man?" the cab driver asks.

I pull my attention away from Libby and shake my head.

"No, I changed my mind." I give him directions back to my place.

When I get home, I change into a pair of sweats and a T-shirt, then head out for a run. I need to get out some of the rage coursing through me. I know that if I don't get rid of it I'm liable to do something completely stupid, like go to Libby's apartment, kidnap her, bring her back to my place, and tie her to the bed until she forgets all about stupid fucking Walter.

∽

Two days later, I'm parked in front of Princess Pizza and wondering what the hell I'm doing. The last two days have been hell. I haven't slept and barely ate. I've spent most of my time trying to convince myself that if Libby is over me, then I need to get over her. But no matter what I say to myself, I can't do it. I'm in love with her, and it's time that I prove that by fighting for us. I called my mom this afternoon and asked her what time the party was this evening. Paying the cab driver, I get out and head into the pizzeria.

The space looks completely different from the last time I was here. The walls have been painted two different shades of pink, and there are new tables with black tops and chrome seats. Colorful framed paintings hanging around the room look like they were done by little kids. Fairy-tale castles, dragons, princesses and princes, horses and unicorns. I pull my eyes off the new art on the walls and scan all the happy faces in the room. I have no idea how the fuck I talked myself into this.

Right . . . for Libby.

My eyes zero in on her as soon as she steps away from an older gentleman. My heart starts to pound hard against my rib cage. She looks beautiful tonight. She's wearing a long black dress that's tied at her waist. Her dark hair is down around her shoulders, and her face is made up almost like it was the night I took her out for our first date. I pull in a few deep breaths to build up the courage I need to do this.

She must sense my eyes on her, because her gaze comes directly to me. Her eyes widen, then fill with worry and fear.

"Antonio." I hear her whisper my name even over the noise in the room. It feels like time stops as we do nothing but stare at each other.

Without telling my feet to do it, I take a step toward her. My hands start to shake. Out of the corner of my eye, I see Walter standing with a group of people. I turn to glare at him, ignoring the knowing grin he's wearing before I return my attention to Libby.

"Antonio. What are you doing here?"

"We're at the part where I need to beg for your forgiveness," I say.

Her body goes still, and even her breathing seems to stop. Closing the distance between us, I go to her and get down on my knees. I take both her hands in mine. I don't give a fuck that everyone in the room has stopped talking. All I care about is the woman in front of me.

"There's this guy. He met a girl, a perfect girl. The perfect girl for him, and he was a jerk to her."

"Antonio." Her eyes close as her hands start to shake, so I hold her more firmly.

"That girl hopefully fell in love with that guy—despite the fact that he doesn't deserve her."

"She did." Her eyes open to meet mine.

"That guy was an idiot." I shake my head. "He was self-centered, selfish, and in the end, an even bigger jerk to the girl. He should have taken better care of her." Tears start to fill her beautiful eyes. "He probably made her cry a lot."

"He did," she tells me. "He also made me drink a lot," she says with a shy smile.

"I hate that, Princess," I whisper. "I hate that I made you cry. I hate that I fucked up. I hate that I walked away from you." My throat starts to get tight with emotion. "I'm so sorry, Princess. So fucking sorry that I didn't listen when you tried to talk to me. Sorry that I didn't trust you the way that I should have. I love you, Libby. Please forgive me for being an asshole."

"I'm sorry, too, you know," she says as tears start to track down her cheeks. "And of course I forgive you. It's my job to take you back even when I shouldn't."

She whispers the last part, and I bury my face against her stomach while I wrap my arms tightly around her waist. Her body curls around mine, and her mouth rests against the top of my head.

"I love you, Antonio."

"I love you, too, Princess. So fucking much." I stand and gather her tightly against my chest when I hear her sob and feel her tuck her face into my neck.

"Show's over," someone says loudly.

I pick her up and carry her to the office, through the crowd of people. I kick the door shut with my foot once we're inside. I don't look around to see the changes she's made; I just take a seat on the couch and hold her in my lap, running my hand up and down her back.

"Princess Pizza?" I mutter.

She giggles, and the sound slides over me, smoothing out all the jagged edges the last two weeks have cut into me.

"I'm in love with a guy who calls me Princess, so I thought it was the perfect name for the shop," she says.

I look at her smiling face.

God, I love her so fucking much.

"Walter can't have you," I growl without thinking, tightening my hold on her.

"What?" She frowns, and the small smile on her face just moments ago disappears with my statement.

"You're mine."

"I know I'm yours," she agrees. "Why are you even talking about Walter?"

"I saw you with him."

"You saw me with him?" she repeats, looking confused. "He's here with Palo."

"Not tonight. A few days ago. I saw you with him here at the shop. You were coming out, and he was with you."

"Oh . . ." Realization fills her beautiful eyes.

"He can't have you," I repeat.

Her eyes soften as her hand comes to rest against my jaw.

"He was just checking on me. The last time he saw me, I had just gotten my heart ripped out of my chest, remember? He was worried, but we're not . . ." She shakes her head. "I wouldn't. I don't want anyone but you."

Hearing that, I close my eyes. "I thought . . ."

"Never," she states firmly. Our eyes lock. "I don't want to be with anyone else but you."

"I can't believe you love me."

"Well, I do. So don't be an idiot. Walter is just a friend and nothing more."

"A friend?" I grumble, and she laughs.

"Yes, he's a friend."

"Are you saying I might have to see him more than just tonight?"

"He lives in LA. I doubt you will see him much, but he's a nice guy. You'd like him if you got to know him."

"I don't think I like that."

"Do you love me?" she asks softly, running her hand through my hair.

I focus on her. "More than anything in the world."

"Then you'll deal."

"If I have to," I agree reluctantly as I study the way her hair is sliding over her shoulder. "I've missed you, Princess. These last two weeks have been hell."

"You could have ended that torture at any time."

"I should have swallowed my pride and come to you sooner. I'm sorry that I didn't listen when you tried to talk to me. I'm sorry that I kept shutting you down when you brought up the shop."

"Are you going to be okay with me owning the shop?" she asks, sounding nervous.

I skim my fingers down the side of her face.

"It's going to take time for me to wrap my head around you owning the shop, and we are going to have to talk about things," I tell her.

She goes rigid on my lap.

"What do you mean, talk about things?" She kind of turns, and it feels like she is going to get up, but I just force her back down.

"What I mean is that I will not sit back and see this place take over your life—*our* life. I will not sit back and watch it pull you down."

"Antonio . . . ," she says softly. This time her hand comes out and cups my face. "I promise you, here and now, that I will never put this place before you. I promise that you and I will come before Princess Pizza."

"When we have kids . . . ," I murmur, ignoring her eyes getting big and her body tensing.

"When are we having kids?"

"I have no idea. But when we do—" I start to say as she puts her fingers on my lips.

"When we do have kids, my main focus will be them. Always," she tells me. "I'm just happy you're here now," she says, then her eyes drop to my mouth. "You know you've forgotten a big part of your apology."

"What's that?"

"In the movies, the guy always—but always—kisses the girl when she forgives him."

"Then I'd better get to that part." I slant my head and kiss her long and hard, so long that at least five different people knock on the door before we finally stop making out. And when we go back out to her party, we do it hand in hand.

Chapter 17

MAYBE ROMANCE MOVIES AREN'T SO STUPID AFTER ALL

LIBBY

"Figured I'd find you in here," Peggy says as she steps into the office.

I look up at her with a sheepish smile.

"Sorry." I set down the phone I just hung up. "I got a call about a party and had to take it. I'm coming—I just need to add the booking into the computer." I pull up the program on my laptop, then look at her again. "Can you tell everyone I'll be out in a minute?"

"It's New Year's Eve and people are still calling to set up reservations?"

"Yes, and we are not going to complain about it, either."

"Hector and I both got Christmas bonuses. If it sounded like I was complaining, you misheard me," she says. I grin at her. "Anyway, I'll let everyone know that you'll be out soon." She smiles before she shuts the door behind herself.

I quickly add the booking for a birthday into the computer, then lean back in my chair and stretch my arms over my head.

It's been almost one year since Princess Pizza opened, and in that time, the shop has paid for itself. It's been so busy that I had to hire three more employees to help out between Friday and Sunday nights. It hasn't hurt that we've even been featured in the *Times*, the *New Yorker*, and a couple of other smaller papers around the city. People from all over the five boroughs come here to celebrate their kids' birthdays and are constantly giving recommendations to their friends and families. The make-your-own-pizza parties have become a hit, and we've been booked almost every weekend since opening.

Antonio and I are also doing amazing—so amazing that just a week ago we decided it was time to stop traveling between his place and mine and move in together. Right now we're looking at condos in his neighborhood, but honestly I don't care where we live as long as I get to go to sleep with him at night and wake up with him in the morning.

Hearing the sound of music start up, I clear my head and smile as I head for the door. Tonight we're closing the shop early to celebrate the New Year. Unfortunately, Antonio has to work, so I won't get to ring it in with him, but my friends are here—along with my parents, my sisters, their husbands, and my nephew. It will still be a night to remember.

When I make it to the front of the shop and see everyone standing around wearing funny hats and silly glasses, I smile.

"You need a hat, too," Fawn says, coming up to me and handing me a top hat with the words New Year's written all over it in gold writing.

I take it from her, then reach out to rub my hand against her round stomach. "Are you feeling okay?"

"Yep." She pulls in a deep breath. "I can't wait until she gets here."

"I can't wait, either," I agree, and she rolls her eyes.

"You just want to be able to shop for her."

"True." I don't deny it. I have loved shopping for my nephew, but girls' clothes are so much cuter than boys'.

"When are you and Antonio going to start?" she asks, studying me.

I shift on my heels. "I don't know." Antonio and I have talked about kids. We know we want them and know that we want at least two, but right now we are just enjoying our time together. And I don't want to have any babies until I have a ring on my finger. Call me old-fashioned.

"You guys will make beautiful babies," she says after a moment, when I don't say more.

"You sound like Mom."

"Oh god." Her nose scrunches up in horror. "I do sound like Mom."

Laughing, I shake my head at her, then feel my lips soften into a smile when Mac comes over with my adorable nephew, Dustin. Taking him from her, I cuddle him to my chest and kiss the top of his tiny head, which is covered in a thin cap.

"Baby looks good on you." Mac grins.

"Whatever." I roll my eyes, then kiss the top of Dustin's head again. I can't stop myself. "I should probably give him back to you before Mom or Martina sees me," I say. Both Fawn and Mac laugh. "It would be funny, but I'm not joking."

Both Martina and my mother have gone from gently questioning Antonio and me about our plans to straight-up harassing us about getting married and starting a family of our own.

"Two minutes until midnight!" I hear Hector shout.

I look over to see Peggy start to fill glasses with champagne.

"Here. I'm going to get a drink." I hand Dustin back to Mac after kissing his head once more, then I hug both of my sisters. "I love you guys."

"Love you, too," they say in unison.

I smile as I let them go. I watch Fawn go to Levi, who tucks her under his arm as soon as she's close. Then I watch Mac curl herself against Wesley, who says something to make her smile before kissing the top of her head. Seeing both my sisters with their guys, my heart fills with happiness for them. Still, I wish Antonio were here.

"One minute!" Hector yells as I grab a glass of champagne and take a sip.

A cool breeze fills the room, meaning someone opened the front door. I turn to see who's coming in. My body freezes when I see Antonio walk in and start toward me, his uniform on and his radio on his collar. I look past him and see that his whole squad is with him.

"What are you doing here?" I ask.

He smiles, wrapping one hand around my back while the other cups the back of my head.

"I couldn't let you ring in the New Year without me. So I traded favors with the guys, and we all came."

He drops his mouth to mine and kisses me deep and wet. People start to count down from ten around us. When he pulls his mouth away and everyone yells, "Happy New Year," my eyes flutter open to meet his. I look around to see everyone hugging and kissing. I take in the moment for just a second.

I did this.

I look back at Antonio, and whether he wants to admit it or not, he helped me more than he knows.

"Happy New Year." I lean up on the tips of my toes and try to kiss him again, but he pulls back before I can, making me frown.

"Princess . . ." He lifts my left hand in his and slowly slides a beautiful solitaire diamond ring onto my finger. "Will you spend this year— and the rest of your life—with me?"

"What?" I breathe, not believing that I heard him correctly even though I know I did. Even though I can feel the weight of the ring he just slid onto my finger. Moving my eyes from his to the ring, I blink in shock. "What?"

I listen to him laugh.

"Put the guy out of his misery," I hear one of the firefighters say.

I look at his squad. They're all watching.

My family and my sisters are smiling while they wipe tears from the corners of their eyes. Their husbands hug them from behind while they kiss their necks.

"What do you say, Princess? Feel like adding a few more chapters to our story?" he asks.

I toss myself against him, wrapping my arms around his neck.

This time, with my own tears falling, I answer, "Yes."

I laugh when I hear a loud cheer go up around us. His squad members high-five one another, and my sisters throw their hands up in celebration.

"Yes," I repeat against his lips, smiling. "Maybe romance movies aren't so stupid after all," I say.

He tips his head to the side, and his laughing mouth covers mine and then kisses me again—this time deeper than before.

～

Holding my hand out in front of me, I watch how the early-morning light coming through the open blinds bounces off my engagement ring.

I'm engaged.

I still can't believe that I'm marrying the guy whom I secretly crushed on for ages. Not only that . . . he loves *me.*

"Morning, Princess." Antonio's rough voice greets me in my ear.

I smile, pressing my back into him as his hand slides up my thigh and over my bare hip.

"Morning." I turn to look at him over my shoulder. I study his mussed hair, his eyes still soft from sleep, and his jaw covered in a thick layer of stubble.

God, I love him so much. More than I ever thought possible.

"You okay?" He kisses my bare shoulder, and I smile.

"More than okay," I answer as his warm hand covers my breast.

He smiles right before he tugs my nipple hard enough to send a jolt of pleasure straight through me.

"How okay?" he asks.

I turn in his arms and slide my hands up his chest, then push him to his back. Climbing on top of him, I look at his handsome face.

"Better than okay," I breathe.

He wraps one hand around his cock and the other around my hip. Feeling the head of him at my entrance, I brace myself with my hands against his chest. My head falls back as I start to slowly sink down onto his length.

"Way better than okay."

I go still with him deep inside me for a moment, to soak in the feeling of our connection. He chuckles, and my eyes open to meet his. He groans.

"So fucking beautiful."

The tone of his voice fills me with a sense of power, and I lift up and then drop, slow and steady, before speeding up and riding him hard and fast, slamming myself down onto him.

Sliding his hands up my stomach, he cups my breasts. He leans up to take one of my breasts into his mouth while toying with the nipple on the other. My eyes close, and a quiet yes leaves my mouth as I slide closer to the edge.

"Christ," he grunts, thrusting his hips up into mine every time I fall down along his length. "So wet . . . so pretty taking my cock."

"Oh god," I whimper when his hand at my breast slides down over my stomach and his thumb starts to roll over my clit.

"Kiss me, Princess," he orders.

My head falls forward, and our eyes lock. I lean closer to him, and my hair cascades down around us. I place my mouth against his and kiss him, coming hard. Before I'm down from the high of my orgasm—or even close to recovering—he flips me to my back, never leaving me. Wrapping my legs around his waist, I hold on to his shoulders as he slams into me over and over, so hard that my breath hitches. Feeling my stomach start to get tight and my muscles start to spasm once more, I cry out.

"Touch yourself," he orders.

Without having the capacity to think about what he's telling me to do, I slide my hand between us and feel our connection as my fingers skim over my clit. My pussy tightens around his length, and my back arches off the bed.

"Antonio!" I cry out as I come again.

I listen to him groan as he falls over the edge with me. His head drops to my shoulder, and I feel his lips when he turns his head to kiss my neck.

Breathing heavy, I soak in the feeling of his weight on top of me and our hearts pounding in unison. I hold him even tighter.

"I love my fiancée's pussy."

My eyes fall closed once more, and my legs and arms spasm as I laugh. "She loves your cock."

"I think I figured that out when she tried to break it off."

"I did *not* try to break it off," I say through my laugher as he leans back to look at me smiling.

"Felt like you were trying to break it off."

"Are you complaining?" I narrow my eyes, and his smile softens. He rolls us over again so I'm on top, then he runs his fingers through my hair.

"I'd never complain about the way you fuck me. I think I saw stars that time."

"Whatever," I grumble.

His body shakes as he starts to laugh.

I can't hold back my smile.

"You're *marrying* me," he says suddenly, the humor leaving his voice. My throat starts to get tight. "Libby Moretti. I really fucking like the sound of that."

"Me, too," I whisper, leaning up and touching my mouth to his. "We're getting married," I say when I pull my mouth from his and his expression softens.

"We are."

"How long do you think we have before our moms start pounding on the door, demanding to know when and where?" I ask, resting my head against his chest.

"Since my mom texted this morning before the sun was even up, I'd say not long."

"Didn't think so."

I smile as I feel his fingers trail lightly down my spine.

"We can elope," he suggests.

I pull away to look down at him and frown. "No way."

"So Vegas is out of the question?"

"Vegas isn't even an option. I want a dress—a big, puffy dress. And a church. I want my dad to walk me down the aisle, and I want to see you waiting for me at the end of that aisle. Where you tell me I'm the most beautiful person you have ever seen. Where we promise to love each other in front of our families."

"Whatever you want, Princess." He grins, wrapping his hand around the back of my neck and pulling me forward for another kiss.

When I lean back and look into his eyes, I can tell that he will always do whatever he can to make me happy. We both might have been tossed around a few times, but in the end, we caught each other. That's all that matters.

Epilogue

ANTONIO

One year later

Watching my wife from across the room, smiling at something Palo is saying to her, my chest fills with pride, love, and possessiveness. Six months after I asked her to marry me, we had a small ceremony at a church in the city. The event was elegant and classy, and I surprised Libby that day with a horse-and-carriage ride to the church to give her a little more of her fairy tale. I've learned over the last year and a half that my wife might like nice things, but she doesn't do over the top unless over the top can be done on a budget. She's perfect for me in every way. I couldn't be luckier.

"Two minutes till midnight!" someone yells.

Libby's eyes find mine across the space.

I close the distance between us while grabbing a beer for myself and picking up a glass of champagne for her off the table.

"Have I told you how beautiful you look?" I ask when her front is tucked against mine and she smiles up at me.

"You might have mentioned it a time or two." She takes the glass of champagne I hand her and holds it down at her side.

"I really love this dress." My eyes roam over the tight red dress that hugs every beautiful inch of her frame while my hand slides around her hip to her back, pulling her closer to me.

"You mentioned that as well." Her fingers dig into my sides as she grabs hold of my shirt.

"One minute!" Hector calls out into the roomful of people.

It's our friends and family—a group of people that has seemed to grow over the last year.

"As much as I love it, I really can't wait to take you home and get you out of it," I whisper against her ear, feeling her shiver.

"Ten!" people start to count around us.

"Five . . . ," I say as I lower my mouth to hers.

"One . . . Happy New Year!" everyone shouts while I kiss my wife.

She pulls her mouth from mine, and I watch her eyes as they open.

"Happy New Year, Daddy."

Those four words spoken against my lips cause my lungs to tighten—along with my grasp on her.

"You're pregnant?" I search her gaze as I stare down at her in disbelief.

"Yes." She smiles as she nods.

Picking her up off the ground, I spin her around in a circle and listen to her laugh. "We're pregnant?"

"Yes." I watch her nod again as tears fill her beautiful eyes. "Are you happy?"

"God, yes." I gather her against me and feel my throat close. I never would have guessed that the woman in my arms would give me everything I ever needed and then some. That she would show me what love is, show me that it's okay to trust another person, show me that it's okay to go after my own dreams.

"Love you, baby," I whisper.

"I love you, too," she whispers back, looking into my eyes.

She does love me. How or why, I don't know. But I'm one lucky guy.

Seven years later

ANTONIO

"Like this, Daddy?"

I look down at my beautiful daughter, Esmeralda, and smile.

"Yeah, baby. Just like that," I encourage as she presses out a ball of dough onto the flat metal surface. Her hair—the same color as her mom's—is tied back in a ponytail. Her tongue is sticking out of her mouth.

"Are you going to teach me how to toss it in the air?" she asks hopefully.

I laugh.

"Do you want me to teach you how to toss it in the air?"

"Yeah! That's the funniest part."

"All right." I pick up a pizza dough that I have already pressed out and toss it into the air, showing her how to do it. Then I watch her try with an amused smile on my face.

"Mommy, look," Esmeralda says. I turn my eyes to my wife and watch her walk toward us. Seeing the look in her eyes, I find it almost hard to breathe. Dropping my eyes to our daughter, I watch her toss the ball of dough into the air and twirl it around.

"If you get any better at that, honey, I'm going to put you to work." Libby smiles at our girl before resting her hand against my arm. Looking down into her eyes, I smile. Then I drop my mouth to hers for a quick kiss.

"I thought you were supposed to be taking the day off . . . ," I say. She rolls her eyes.

"I slept in. I'm okay now," she says.

I move my eyes to her stomach. She's nine months pregnant, and this pregnancy has been harder on her than the last.

"You need to be home, Princess. You need to rest."

"I want to be here, spending time with my family," she counters.

I sigh, knowing I'm fighting a losing battle. She loves the pizzeria. It's her baby, too, and dragging her away from it is like pulling teeth.

"We will all go home together as soon as our pizzas are done."

"I have some stuff to take care of in the office."

"Don't make me talk to Hector," I whisper.

She narrows her eyes. The week after she found out she was pregnant with Esmeralda, she offered Hector and Marco part of Princess Pizza. Even though it was her baby, she knew they would love and care for it just as much as she did. So they worked it out where the three of them would each work a couple of days a week and hire extra people to help take over. Now my wife only works two days a week and does most of the paperwork.

"Fine. We'll all go home when the pizzas are done," she gives in.

I fight back a smile, knowing she won't like that much.

"Don't pout, Princess. I'm just worried about you and our boy."

"I know," she agrees quietly, rubbing her belly, my son no doubt kicking up a storm.

Placing another soft kiss on her lips, we turn our attention to our daughter. We watch her toss her pizza dough into the air and spin it around before she puts her toppings on it and I place it in the oven.

~

"Oh god!" Libby cries, tucking her face against my chest.

I pull my eyes from the TV and frown. She's never scared when we're watching scary movies.

"It's happening."

"What?" I pull her face away from my chest and look into her wide eyes.

"I . . ." She stops and clutches her hands to her stomach.

I feel my eyes widen. "Shit." I get off the couch and lean down over her. "Breathe, baby."

"I'm breathing." Her mouth pinches, and her eyes fill with worry. "I feel . . . he's coming."

"I'm going to get Esmeralda up and grab the bag. Just stay here and breathe," I order.

She nods.

"Be right back." I place a quick kiss on the top of her head, then run for Esmeralda's room. I turn on the light so I don't kill myself by tripping over one of the toys scattered across her bedroom floor.

"Daddy . . ."

"You need to get up and get dressed, baby. Mommy's going to be having your brother soon," I tell her.

A beautiful smile lights up her face before she bounds from her bed and starts to rush around her room.

Knowing she's getting ready, I head for the master suite and grab Libby's hospital bag from the closet. I toss it on the bed before I grab a pair of jeans and put them on, then grab a shirt and put that on, too. Dressed, I grab some clothes for Libby and head back out to the living room.

She's now kneeling on the couch, with her face tucked into a pillow.

"Something's wrong," she whimpers, lifting her head. "You should call an ambulance."

"We'll make it to the hospital faster than an ambulance can get here, Princess," I tell her, smoothing her hair away from her damp forehead.

She shakes her head.

"No, he's coming. I can feel him."

"You can feel him . . . ," I repeat as my stomach sinks.

"Yes!" she cries as she tucks her face back into the couch, her body arching awkwardly.

Seeing the amount of pain she's in, I quickly call 911. I hang up when they tell me they are on the way.

"Antonio, he's coming!"

"It's going to be okay, Princess." I pull her pants down over her hips and almost pass out when I see the crown of my son's head. "Fuck." I rush to the bathroom and grab some towels, then go back to her and help her move to her back.

"Daddy . . . ?" Esmeralda's worry-filled voice fills the otherwise-silent room.

I look at our girl, who's standing in the hall.

"It's okay, baby. I need you to get me a bowl of warm water," I tell her. She runs to the kitchen.

"I'm so scared, Antonio," Libby whispers.

My eyes lock with hers.

"It's going to be okay," I assure her, tucking some towels under her bottom. "An ambulance is on the way."

I know they won't make it in time—our boy is almost here. "Push if you feel like you need to push," I encourage as she pants.

Seeing her nod, I pray that I can remember everything I learned in training.

"Oh god." She curls around her stomach.

I hold her legs open and feel my heart thunder against my rib cage as our son's head appears.

"The baby is crowning," I say to her.

When Esmeralda comes back with a bowl of water, I take it. "Go wait by the door, baby. An ambulance will be here soon. When they get here, just let them in."

"Is Mommy okay?" she asks.

"I'm okay, honey." Libby gives her a tight smile, then closes her eyes as another contraction rips through her. A long groan comes out of her.

"Go, baby."

"Okay," Esmeralda whispers before running off to the front door.

"I need to push again," Libby whimpers in pain. "It's coming, Antonio," she says to me, fear filling her eyes.

"It's okay, Princess. Push. You're doing so good." I rub her thigh. Looking down between her legs, I see our son's head coming out a bit more.

"I'm so scared," she says, panting.

"I know, baby. But I promise it's going to be okay." I try to keep my voice calm, but my body is almost shaking in fear. "I need you to bear down. You can do it."

"Okay." Her eyes close tight as she curls herself around her stomach once more. I wrap my hands around our son's head and let out a sigh of relief when his shoulders slide out, then the rest of his body. I quickly wrap him in a clean dry towel and settle him against her chest. The sound of his wails now fills the room as my wife holds him.

"He's so beautiful." She looks at me, quietly sobbing.

"They're here!" Esmeralda yells from the front door.

I look at my wife and see her eyes on our son.

"They're here!" Esmeralda runs into the room, followed by two paramedics.

"Good job, baby," I tell her.

She smiles at me before going to her mom and resting her head next to her brother's on Libby's chest. Libby opens up her arms so she can hold our children together.

Seeing my family all together—healthy, alive, and breathing—I know that everything will be okay.

Years later

MISS INA

"Grandma Ina, can you tell me a story?" Olivia, Fawn and Levi's daughter, asks as she comes over to sit next to me on the couch.

I smile down at the sweet girl. I tried to tell all the children's mothers that I didn't want to be called Grandma Ina, but like always, they ignored me. I will never admit it to anyone, but I do love it. Especially since I don't have grandchildren of my own to spoil.

"What story would you like me to tell you, dear?"

"The one about Mommy and Daddy."

"Oh, I want to hear the story of my mommy and daddy," Esmeralda says excitedly, coming over to take a seat next to her cousin.

"I don't want to hear about my mom and dad. I already have to see them kissing and stuff. It's so gross," Dustin, Mackenzie and Wesley's son, says, making a face that has my lips twitching.

Still, he doesn't leave—he even gets a little closer when I start.

Quietly, I tell them the stories of how each of their parents found love, then end softly with what I say every time they ask to hear the story: "Whether you run into it, stumble into it, or get tossed into it, love has a way of finding you."

"I hope love finds me one day. I want to marry a prince," Olivia says with a dreamy sigh.

"I want to marry a policeman," Esmeralda says with a grin. "That way I can shoot his gun."

Oh dear.

"I never want to get married. Girls are gross," Dustin complains.

Both his cousins look at him with narrowed eyes.

"Girls are not gross. *Boys* are gross. They stink," Olivia says, getting off the couch.

"Yeah, and they do weird stuff like eat glue," Esmeralda adds.

"I don't smell or eat glue," Dustin says, defending his gender.

I start to laugh. Yes, I do love this. I'm lucky to have had a chance to experience the beauty of love and family even after thinking I never would again . . .

But, like I said, love happens when you least expect it. Even to old women.

Acknowledgments

First, I have to give thanks to God, because without Him, none of this would be possible. Second, I want to thank my husband. I love you now and always—thank you for believing in me even when I don't believe in myself. To my beautiful son, you bring such joy into my life. I'm so honored to be your mom.

To every blogger and reader, thank you for taking the time to read and share my books. There would never be enough ink in the world to acknowledge you all, but I will forever be grateful to each and every one of you.

I started this writing journey after I fell in love with reading, like thousands of authors before me. I wanted to give people a place to escape, where the stories were funny, sweet, hot, and left you feeling good. I have loved sharing my stories with you all, loved that I have helped people escape the real world, even for a moment.

I started writing for me, but I will continue writing for you.

XOXO Aurora

About the Author

Aurora Rose Reynolds is a *New York Times* and *USA Today* bestselling author whose wildly popular series include Until, Until Him, Until Her, and Underground Kings.

Her writing career started in an attempt to get the outrageously alpha men who resided in her head to leave her alone, and it has blossomed into an opportunity to share her stories with readers all over the world.

For more information on Reynolds's latest books or to connect with her, contact her on Facebook at www.facebook.com/AuthorAuroraRoseReynolds, on Twitter @Auroraroser, or via email at Auroraroser@gmail.com. To order signed books and find out the latest news, visit her at www.AuroraRoseReynolds.com or https://www.goodreads.com/Auroraroser.